RACHEL FORD

RHAPSODY OF LOVE

D0524151

Complete and Unabridged

LINFORD
Leicester

First published in 1990 in Great Britain

First Linford Edition
published 2006

British Library CIP Data

Ford, Rachel
  Rhapsody of love / Rachel
  Ford
Ford Rhapsody of love of the novel—
  Rl
  Li
  1. Love stories   LP
  2. Large type books
  I. Title
  82 1494213

  ISBN 1–84617–146–6

Published by
F. A. Thorpe (Publishing)
Anstey, Leicestershire

Set by Words & Graphics Ltd.
Anstey, Leicestershire
Printed and bound in Great Britain by
T. J. International Ltd., Padstow, Cornwall

This book is printed on acid-free paper

RHAPSODY OF LOVE

When painter Maggie Sanderson found herself trapped in the same Caribbean hideaway as world-famous composer Steve Donellan, she was at a loss what to do. She tried to distance herself from him, but he seemed determined to make his presence felt, crashing his way around the house day and night. Was there no way she could find peace from this man, or was he going to ruin her sanity too, as he had ruined everything else?

For Tony
who has put up with
a 'Gemini' wife for years
with no complaints —
well, not too many!

1

Well — bye then, Maggie. Thanks for everything. See you around . . .

Was this the way love-affairs always ended, even after six years? So civilised — but then, David always had been civilised. No hassle, no hard feelings, no bones broken. Hearts, though, were a different matter . . .

He'd edged his way past her easel, ultra-carefully so as not to smudge the still-wet print, paused in the doorway and turned. For one dreadful moment she'd thought he had been about to offer to shake hands — that she really could not have borne. But then he'd swung round and as she'd stood motionless she'd heard his footsteps, slow at first then more lightly, pattering down the stairs, and at last the click as the front door to the flats had closed behind him . . .

That had been five weeks, three days, four hours ago, and here she was yet again walking — walking for mile after unseeing mile through parts of London she'd barely known existed; drifting in and out of shops, across parks where regimented rows of narcissi and tulips waved stiffly in the raw April breeze, and now here through this bustling street market. People, people all round her — the vendors, a dozen different nationalities, shouting their wares, the crowds, hurrying, pushing her unresistingly against a fruit stall.

'You wan' yam, papaw, miss?'

The voice, the accent, warm and brown and comforting as creamy cocoa . . . From a long way off, memories came tugging at her.

'What?'

She stared stupidly at the stout, dusky-skinned woman in tightly buttoned coat and flowered hat.

'Bombay mango — ripe, jus' ready for eating, miss.'

Obediently, Maggie took the coral-flushed fruit which the woman was holding out enticingly, and as she cradled it between her chill hands its honeyed fragrance rose to her.

Moon Creek . . . The white-washed façade of the old house dreaming in the afternoon heat . . . The ancient, gnarled mango trees in the garden behind, dropping their ripe fruit . . . For a fleeting instant the drab London street market and the grey April afternoon faded and she was back at her grandmother's lovely house on the tiny West Indian island of St Hilaire.

Then — of course. That was what she'd do. She was only surprised it had taken her so long.

'Yes,' she said aloud, and for the first time in nearly six weeks her taut features softened into a half-smile. 'I'll go back — back to St Hilaire.'

2

'Want something?'

Maggie, who had been cautiously craning her neck, hoping to catch the first glimpse of St Hilaire ahead, jerked back abruptly as she met the chill dark blue eyes of the man sitting next to her.

'I-I'm sorry?'

'Do you want something?' The man's tone was not encouraging.

'N-no.' Hastily, she shrank back into her seat, colouring with embarrassment. 'I was only — '

But he had already turned away to bury himself once again in the copy of *Newsweek* he had been engrossed in since they had left Kingston.

Maggie directed a quick scowl at his unconscious profile, then, still flushed, determinedly fixed her eyes on the seat in front of her. What a charmer. Her fellow passengers must have known

4

something she didn't, to leave this the one vacant seat on the small jet she'd scrambled headlong on to, after her British Airways flight from London had been delayed by turbulence in mid-Atlantic.

After a few minutes, though, she shot him another glance out of the extreme corner of her eye, surreptitiously at first, then with growing confidence as he continued to be totally absorbed in his magazine. He was certainly good-looking, she had to give him that. A profile saved from pure film star perfection only by a certain hard-edged quality and a slightly blunted nose. An accident? No, more likely in his case a fight. But under that thatch of straw-coloured hair it was a handsome face none the less: those sloe-blue eyes, dark almost to the point of blackness; thick lashes shading the wide cheekbones; the mouth wide, and — she leaned forward a fraction to trace its outline with her eyes — surprisingly sensitive.

All in all, quite a face. Although she

hadn't done a portrait for at least three years, she found herself viewing him as a prospective subject. Of course, it would be difficult to capture those shades and nuances of character. It was a carefully schooled face, she sensed, in which far more lay hidden than was revealed on that hard-planed, uncompromising surface . . .

What was he? She wrinkled her snub nose slightly as she tried to puzzle it out. American — New England, perhaps, from his accent, mid-thirties — a man of action surely. She sensed that, an elbow's width from her, there was a tensed-up energy, coiled and kept carefully just under control. An oil man, on his way back to Trinidad or Caracas, perhaps. Or maybe a yacht hand — no, the skipper, she hastily corrected herself; this man didn't look like anybody's *hand* — en route to pick up his latest charter.

She caught herself up, unable to suppress a little shamefaced smile. Here she was, indulging in the same childish game she'd always played while on flights to and from the island — studying total strangers, trying to penetrate the anonymous features to guess at the occupation, the personality behind. And this had been long before she'd realised that the urge to see beyond the superficial skin and bone structure to the real person within had been leading her inexorably towards her own vocation . . .

She became aware of the faint, but still intimidating frown, as the yachtsman cum oil rig worker next to her clearly sensed her eyes on him, and instantly she abandoned her character-reading in favour of once more studying the fabric of the seat in front.

Her legs were beginning to ache. She flexed them as much as she could in the confined space, wriggling her toes and wishing yet again that she'd worn sandals instead of trainers and, as a trickle of sweat meandered down from hair to fine hair on her thighs, that she'd opted for a dress rather than these heavy cotton dungarees.

But when, the previous day, she'd dug out her summer clothes from the bottom of the wardrobe, she'd made the demoralising discovery that every one of them was too tight. That fatal combination of junk food and, at least since just before David had walked out, endless bars of chocolate to assuage, if only temporarily, her misery, had deposited inches and pounds all over her once slender frame where they simply had no business to be.

Even these pink dungarees were already tight, and she'd only bought them a month ago. And buying them had in itself been pretty traumatic. After a frantic struggle, she'd reluctantly had to accept that thirty-six-inch hips were an impossibility. Being French, they'd only been labelled in metric sizing, and for some reason 'hanches 97' was — well, altogether even more depressing than '38 hip'. It'd made her feel like a side of beef on a hook. Come to think of it, she probably *looked* like one as well . . .

To stop her thoughts from becoming enmeshed in yet another downward spiral, she automatically reached into her bag for the last of the bars of chocolate she had bought at Heathrow but then, with a rare spurt of will-power, firmly zipped up the bag and glanced instead at her watch.

Surely St Hilaire must be in sight soon, if she could only see it. This was the other secret game she'd always played — trying to spot the green smudge on the horizon before the intercom announcement came.

Her neighbour was now giving his rapt attention to what seemed to be a background feature on the latest scandal to rock Wall Street. But then he put it down on his lap and fished out a pencil and an old envelope from his jacket pocket. Frowning deeply, he began scribbling a series of highly complicated sets of figures.

That was it, then. He was a

stockbroker — down on his luck, though, to judge from the cream lightweight cotton suit, so crumpled that it looked as though it had been slept in.

If she could just . . . Very gently, she craned to see past him — softly — softly . . . A heavy lock of her long red-gold hair swung forward and gently flipped against his ear. He swung round and looked at her as though she were something that had just crawled out of the baggage hold. Screwing the envelope into a tight ball, he snatched up the journal and thrust it at her.

'For Pete's sake — if you're so keen to read it, be my guest.'

She felt her colour rising again but managed to retort haughtily, 'It's quite all right, thank you. I don't want to read it.'

When he raised one elegant eyebrow in infuriating disbelief, she added, 'If you must know, I was just trying to look out of the window, to see if we're nearly there.'

He rolled his eyes in a give-me-strength look of resignation, then, leaning past her, gently tapped the arm of her other neighbour, an elderly nun in tropical whites who had been serenely catnapping since taking off from Palisadoes Airport.

'Pardon us one moment, ma'am. This lady wants to change seats.'

And before Maggie, an angry flush flaring in her cheeks, could protest that she wanted no such thing, she had somehow been propelled into the narrow aisle, the oilman-seadog-failed stockbroker hard on her heels. As she turned, the plane dipped suddenly so that, her feet all pins and needles, she stumbled back, first landing heavily on his foot, then, as the plane righted itself, cannoning sharply against him.

Instinctively she threw up her hands, steadying herself against his chest. For one moment she stood, her fingers splayed, feeling beneath her palms the slow, regular beat of his heart under the hard chest muscles. Sitting down, she simply hadn't realised how tall he was, but now he towered over her, so that she found herself engaged in an eyeball-to-eyeball confrontation with the brown V of chest visible under the casually open white shirt.

Her cheeks scarlet now, she backed off with a muttered apology and, hastily shuffling into his vacated seat, shook her hair forward to screen her hot face. Fumbling in her bag for her sunglasses, she jammed them on her nose then turned away to gaze fixedly out of the porthole window beside her.

But when, a few minutes later, she heard the pilot's announcement that they would be landing very shortly at Port Charlotte Airport, shade temperature ninety-two degrees Fahrenheit, she realised with a start that she had been staring wholly unseeingly at those beloved conical blue-green hills, the dense sweep of foliage on the plateau below, and that delicious fringe of pale clotted cream where St Hilaire met the translucent green of the Caribbean.

Around her passengers were chatting animatedly above the bromide Muzak, but Maggie, seeking the familiar landmarks after four years' exile, now gazed out of the window with absolute concentration. When the plane had rolled to a halt the doors were opened, so that the tropical heat billowed in like a soft, enfolding quilt.

As the first passengers began to move, her neighbour was up and away, moving out of his seat and down the aisle with an alacrity which convinced her that he was at least as anxious to be quit of her as she was to see the back of that shaggy fair hair and broad-shouldered frame forever.

★   ★   ★

Maggie had expected that, as she had been the last passenger to board, her two cases would put in an early appearance. Not so. Almost all the others had retrieved their luggage and gone through from the arrivals hall, but still she stood, tapping her foot and torn between impatience and concern. Perhaps her baggage was still sitting on the tarmac at Palisadoes — on the other hand, perhaps it was in the hold of that Avianca jet which had been noisily revving up en route for Bogota . . .

A small cluster of luggage lurched into sight on the conveyor and with a surge of thankfulness she reached out for her two bulging cases — just as a large hand, followed by a horribly familiar cream-cotton arm, shot past her to snatch up a canvas and leather holdall.

Maggie leapt back, jerking the smaller of her cases sharply against the rail, and next instant the catches, uncertain at the best of times, sprang open. As she watched helplessly, a shower of untidily packed clothes spewed out on to the carousel.

'Oh, no!'

Hot and tired, she felt this was the last straw. She all but stamped her foot, then, hurling her case on to the floor, rounded on her tormentor from the plane, her grey eyes storm-dark with temper.

'That was your fault, you — you oaf.' His sudden scowl only incensed her further. 'If you hadn't been in such a hurry, grabbing like an ill-mannered — '

'If I were you, lady,' he chipped in coldly, 'I'd stop bawling like a fishwife and retrieve my possessions.' He leaned across and delicately lifted between finger and thumb a pair of opaque white cotton panties that were just gliding away. 'This — er — garment is yours, I take it?'

Maggie turned an even brighter red, though less from embarrassment at the pants — chosen in her present mood more for tropical comfort than glamour — than fury at the glint of malicious humour in those dark blue eyes.

'Thank you, I'll have those,' she just managed to say through clenched teeth, but then, as he dropped them into her outstretched hands, she became aware that several other garments of an equally intimate nature were revolving gently around on the carousel. She scurried in pursuit, snatching them off, then knelt down and began bundling them back into her case. It just had to be this case, of course, not the other one, which contained her painting materials and other equally innocuous items.

She was just managing to ignore the long cream legs, which she could glimpse from under her red-gold fringe, when she heard what was unmistakably a barely smothered laugh. She tensed for an instant then slowly straightened, drawing herself up to make the most of every precious inch. Even so, she had to tilt her face up to meet his.

'If — ' Rendered momentarily speechless by her anger, she broke off, shooting him instead a laser glare which should have reduced him to a heap of smoking rubble, then somehow found her voice again. 'If you were a gentleman, you'd offer to help instead of behaving like — like — ' her voice rose as she hunted desperately for the right word ' — a *cad*.'

An expression of extreme mirth flickered across the hard face. 'A *cad*?' He frowned as though in serious thought. 'Among all the varied epithets which have been applied to me through the years, I have never been called a cad.' He shook his head reprovingly. 'You know, honey, I do believe you've been reading more romances than are good for you.'

He hunked up his case then, just as he was turning away, she caught, 'Tut, tut. Too many romances, and far too many chocolate bars.'

So he hadn't been as unaware of her and her compulsive eating as he'd appeared to be. Scarlet now with mortification and unable to find a cutting enough retort, she stooped down and quickly threw the last items into her case.

As she closed the lid once more though, she paused. Cad. Whatever in the world had possessed her, modern twenty-seven-year-old woman that she was, to use that old-fashioned term? Because the only suitable alternative was a word which, having been carefully raised by her parents, she tried never to use. Pity, though. It was tailor-made for a brute like him.

She scowled at the doorway through which he had disappeared, then, all at once, as her natural good humour reasserted itself, her lips twitched and she found herself giggling helplessly.

When she came through from customs, the small reception lounge was deserted of passengers. Smilingly refusing the glass of rum punch from the tourist courtesy girl, she pushed open the glass doors and emerged from the super-cool air-conditioning into the shimmering late afternoon heat.

★ ★ ★

She paid off the cab at the top of the track and stood watching as it accelerated off in a spurt of reddish dust, then hitched up her shoulder-bag, picked up her cases and set off. The driver had looked mildly surprised when she'd asked to be set down here, a good half-mile from the house; impossible to explain to him that she wanted to be absolutely alone for her first view of Moon Creek.

Even so, after fifty yards, with the sweat oozing down between her shoulder blades and her arms being slowly pulled none too gently out of their sockets, she began to regret the romantic gesture. But suddenly her breath caught in her throat as, beyond the stone wall and through the gnarled silver-grey cotton trees, spreading mahoganies and palms that enclosed the estate, there was the thread of silver which was Moon River, the blue-green sea and finally the house, tiny in the distance, a pure white and perfect child's toy.

With a little sigh of sheer pleasure, Maggie dumped her cases on the dusty track and, leaning up against the shaggy trunk of the nearest palm, let her mind fill with the vibrant colour and the sounds, all but forgotten for four years but now gloriously, instantly familiar again: the dry whispering from the cane fields over to her right, the plaintive chirrup of an invisible cri-cri bird, and overhead the soft shushing of the palm fronds in the hot breeze.

Screwing up her eyes against the brilliance, she could just make out the veranda, shrouded with flowering creepers, which ran the length of the façade. In half an hour she'd be sitting in the old bamboo rocking-chair, waiting for Adela or one of the maids to bring her a jug of iced lime juice. Bliss. She could almost hear the ice-cubes clinking, see the hot air frosting on the glass . . . Swallowing down her saliva, she eased her shoulders against the tight straps of her dungarees and picked up the cases again.

She was almost up to the tall wrought-iron gates set into the imposing stone wall and pillars before she registered. They were closed. She frowned in puzzlement. But the gates of Moon Creek were never closed; never in her life had she known them other than swung wide like welcoming arms. And when she peered through, she saw that someone had kicked the two prop stones away into the grass.

She was amazed that the hinges, rusting for two hundred years in the salt air, had been made to close at all — she was going to have the devil's own job opening them again. But then, as she put her hand against them, she realised that not only were they tightly closed — they were, for good measure, padlocked with an iron chain.

Its heavy links lay on her palm and she stared down at them, a slight *frisson* of unease running through her. Of course, her globe-trotting grandmother wasn't here — she knew that. But when, still caught up in that impetuous mood which had swept over her in the drab London street market, she'd rung her, catching up with her finally in

Monaco paying a duty visit on Maggie's parents, she had promised to warn the agent who looked after the property that her granddaughter was on her way.

Even so, there'd been *something* in her grandmother's tone — a slight undercurrent that she'd been able to dismiss at the time as a fault in the long-distance line, but which now that she recalled it only added to the growing sense of unease.

She gave the gates a final fierce, unavailing rattle then stepped back and surveyed the stone wall. It was nearly six feet high and ran for some distance in both directions. Her great-grandfather had had it built, though less to fence himself in than to provide work for some of the local men at one of the periodic times of slumping sugar prices, when the fields would be fired or harvested only to produce animal feed.

Oh, well, it was useless standing here, waiting for someone to shout, 'Open Sesame,' and so, leaving her cases where they were, she followed the wall until, after a couple of hundred yards, she found what she was looking for — an enormous cotton tree, its low branches growing right up against the wall.

Hitching up the legs of her dungarees, she scrambled up through the branches and seconds later was half sliding, half crawling down the other side, to land with a plop in the long grass. Closing her mind to any pepper ants or scorpions that might be lurking, she thrust her way through the lush undergrowth until she stood on the rutted driveway, then, brushing away the twigs and leaves which festooned her, she began walking briskly in the direction of the house.

What on earth could have happened? Maybe Joseph, her grandmother's handyman-caretaker, had at last been gently persuaded into retirement, and now a new, younger man was trying to prove how ultra-efficient he was. Whatever the explanation it would turn out to be perfectly reasonable, and Maggie, never able to hold resentment for longer than five minutes, found herself humming softly.

'Hey you. Hold it right there!'

She had not heard the footsteps behind her, and almost leapt out of her skin at the furious shout. Swinging round, at first half blinded by the low sun, she could see nothing but then, putting her hand to her eyes, she could just make out in the dense shade of trees which overhung the path leading up from the beach the darker outline of a man.

Maggie's hackles instantly stood on end. He obviously thought she was an intruder and was only doing his job, but even so . . .

'It's all right,' she called, rather stiffly, but then, as her mouth sagged open with horrified disbelief, she gave a strangled groan.

It couldn't be. But it was. As the man emerged from the shadows, it all too obviously was. He had changed from that cream suit into denim shorts and a towel was slung casually round his shoulders; he'd clearly been swimming, so that his hair was still damp, but even so, there was no mistaking that thick thatch of pale, fawn hair, or the large, hard body with which she had so painfully collided.

He came right up to her then stood, his thumbs hitched into his belt, slowly surveying her in silence. Something about that silence, and the frown which accompanied it, was suddenly very intimidating. Maggie licked her lips and tried to speak, but all words had deserted her.

Finally, the survey complete, an expression of extreme distaste crossed his features. 'I don't believe it. I told myself there had to be a dozen other pairs of well-filled pink dungarees — '

Maggie stiffened in outrage. 'Now look here — '

' — scampering around St Hilaire, but all the time I knew.' The barely controlled fury in his voice only seemed to heighten the Boston drawl. 'Just what the hell are you playing at — are you haunting me or something?'

'I most certainly am not.' She drew herself up. It was all she ever seemed to do when he was around — that, and blush. And she was horribly afraid that even now her cheeks were flushing an unbecoming pink. If only she were *taller*, she railed inwardly. 'I don't know who you are — or who you think you are — '

'And I don't know who the hell you are.'

'I — ' Maggie put her snub nose in the air ' — am Marguerite Sanderson.'

'I don't care if you're the Queen of Sheba. And I don't know what you're doing — apart from haunting me, that is — but you can just get the hell out of here. *Now*.'

She shook her head slightly, to try and clear the paralysing bewilderment. What on earth was going on? He was behaving as though *he* was the owner of Moon Creek, ordering some undesirable off his property — or, at the very least, acting as if he had every right to send her packing.

He couldn't possibly be the new caretaker, or any other employee for that matter. Her grandmother, fiercely loyal to the islanders, would never have taken on an outsider — and certainly not a boorish oaf like this. In any case, this man just did not have the bearing of a servant. So — was she going mad? Or was he? The thought, lightning-swift, ran through her.

'Now look,' she began, her tone all at once more placatory, 'there seems to have been some stupid mix-up. I don't think you quite understand the situation.'

'No. It's *you* that does not understand the situation, so let me make it perfectly clear. You are leaving, right now, the way you came.'

Another thought struck her, and she stared up at him, her eyes narrowing. 'Was it you, by any chance, who locked the gates?'

'Sure. I thought — foolishly — that it would keep the riff-raff out.'

'Well, of all the — '

'So if you'll drop that outraged pouter-pigeon act and get moving — '

'No, I damn well won't. And let me tell you — '

'No, lady,' he cut in, his expression grim, 'let *me* tell *you*. If you are not out of here in ten seconds flat . . . '

The threat was all the worse for being left unfinished, but all her innate stubbornness flared into life. 'Sorry, but I'm not going anywhere.'

Folding her arms, she half turned away and planted her trainers very firmly on the driveway. Behind her defiance, though, she was wondering nervously just what his reaction would be. She did not have long to wait to find out.

With a furious exclamation, he hurled down the towel and seized hold of her by the wrist. Swinging her round, he tightened his grip, bringing her arm sharply up behind her. Terrified now, Maggie let out a yell.

'Help! Help!'

He gave her arm another jerk. 'Save your breath, honey. There's no one to hear you.'

Adela. And the others. Where were they? She strained her ears, but there were no running foot-steps, no reassuring shouts — no sound at all, apart from her laboured breathing. Perhaps if she managed to kick hard enough, she could break free. But then, as she squirmed downwards, she caught a glimpse of his face and decided that, for the moment at least, discretion was the better part of valour.

'Now, move.'

'L-let go. You're breaking my arm.'

'Will you walk, then?'

'Yes,' she muttered through her teeth, and his grip eased to a slightly more comfortable hold.

Tears of helpless rage stung her eyes as she stumbled along in front of him. Just what was she doing, allowing herself to be booted off her own — or, at least, her grandmother's property — by this bullying swine? Never in her entire life had she felt so humiliated. If it took ten years, she'd get even with him.

'You — you just can't do this,' she panted breathlessly.

'But, as you see, I am.'

'You'll be sorry,' she hurled over her shoulder, her voice trembling as she hovered on the edge of tears. 'That's all I'm going to say.'

'Good.'

His hateful voice was in her ear, and she set her teeth on any further speech. She had intended one final attempt to explain — after all, he was the one who was going to look pretty silly in a little while. But she wouldn't lower herself; let him think he'd won, whoever he was.

At the gates he wrenched her round again, then pushed her — fairly gently — up against them. Resting one foot in the wrought-ironwork so that she was trapped between his bare thighs, unable to break free, he dug a key out of his pocket, undid the padlock and swung one of the gates open.

She was still pinioned against the other gate; his warm breath was stirring the tendrils of hair on her forehead and he made no move to release her. Hot and exhausted, all fight knocked out of her, she stood, head bent, shoulders drooping as unpleasant little wavelets of dizzy nausea rippled back and forth inside her.

All at once, she felt a fat tear sliding down her cheek. As it plopped on to her dungarees, she fiercely flicked it away then looked up to catch the tail-end of a glance. Just for an instant she half thought she'd seen a softening of those inexorable blue eyes, but if so, it was soon gone.

'Now — out.'

He propelled her through the narrow gap and, furious with herself for the weakness of that tear, she snatched up her cases and began almost running up the track. As she did so, she heard the click as he relocked the gate.

3

As soon as she was out of sight round the first bend in the track, though, Maggie slowed and then stopped. Dropping her cases, which were beginning to feel as though they had been stuffed with lead bars, she plumped down on the bank.

What on earth was she going to do? Her self-confidence, already so bruised by David's cruel rejection, had now been pummelled almost into oblivion — though not so much by that arrogant swine back there as by the way she had so spinelessly allowed him to manhandle her off Moon Creek, where she had a two-hundred-per-cent right to be.

Perhaps she should head on into Port Charlotte, look up Dawn or one of her other old schoolfriends and stay there while she licked her wounds and worked out her next move. No! She caught herself up sharply. For heaven's sake, was she a woman or a mouse? She'd come to stay at Moon Creek and that was precisely what she was going to do.

First, though, she would go into town and call on Mr Deacon, the estate agent who oversaw the property and acted for her grandmother during her frequent absences from the island. That way, at least she should find out what was going on. Maybe the man was an employee of Mr Deacon, in which case she'd have a thing or two to tell his boss.

Either way, she'd be back in triumph very soon and he'd be grovelling at her feet in abject apology. She smiled to herself with a vindictiveness which quite shocked her, then thrust her cases behind a clump of oleander bushes and, hearing a truck labouring along the road, hared off up the track to try to get a ride into town.

★　★　★

'Good heavens. Maggie.'

'Hi, Phil.'

Maggie shook hands and smiled back at the tall, well-built young St Hilairean, then followed him through to the air-conditioned comfort of his office. She slid into the chair he held for her and watched as he took his place in the big leather swivel-chair behind the desk.

'I see you've finally persuaded your uncle.'

'That Deacon and Reid sounds better than just Deacon, you mean?' He grinned boyishly. 'Yes, it has a certain ring, doesn't it? Best estate agency on the island, though I say it myself.'

'Mmm.' She looked teasingly at him, taking in his crisp white shirt and immaculate grey suit. 'Just look at you — and you were always the tearaway of Port Charlotte Academy.'

'Well, it takes one to spot one. I seem to remember that once upon a time you were the terror of the teachers. Do you remember when you and Cathy Hartley nearly blew up the chemistry lab between you?'

Maggie gave a reminiscent wince. 'Oh, don't, Phil. I certainly can — and the roasting we got from her father afterwards.'

'Anyway, Maggie,' Phil all at once became the brisk young executive, 'it's great to see you again. But we weren't expecting you till next week.'

'No, well, I managed to get an early flight,' she said carefully. Impossible to tell even an old crony like Phil that, in her almost feverish anxiety to be away from London — and those painful memories of David everywhere in the flat they'd shared — she'd snatched barehanded at the first available flight. She paused. 'Gran did tell you I was coming, then?'

'Sure. Mrs Faulkner rang me, oh, a couple of days ago. But I'm afraid Moon Creek may not be ready for you. I was going out there at the weekend to check things over. The tenant's been away for a couple of days but I think he's due back some time today.'

The tenant? Maggie stared at him open-mouthed. 'I didn't know she had a tenant.'

'Oh, yes. Hasn't she told you? She's been letting the house on short leases to tourists for over a year now. Only her part of the house, of course — not your parents' — so I suppose she didn't see any need to tell you.'

'No, I suppose not,' she agreed slowly, then, with dawning trepidation, 'This tenant — who is he? You did say *he*?'

'He's American. Boston Irish, I should think. His name's Steve Donellan.'

'Is he on his own?'

'Yes. No family with him.'

'And what's he like?' Maggie forced herself to ask.

'Oh — ' Phil shrugged vaguely ' — mid-thirties, well-built.'

'Dark-haired, I suppose.' She was still allowing herself to hope.

'No, very fair. Quite a good-looker.' He flashed her an arch look. 'Interested?'

'Certainly not,' Maggie replied, too quickly, but he did not seem to notice.

'It won't be quite the same for you, I'm afraid, having a neighbour. I'm surprised your grandmother didn't tell you.'

'Well, she always was vague — ' Maggie began, then broke off as, abruptly, the memory of that phone conversation surged back. Her grandmother's reaction when she'd said she'd wanted to return to Moon Creek — that funny little laugh, which she'd put down to the bad line, the 'I think that's a very good idea, my pet.' Maggie was suddenly quite certain that her grandmother had known exactly what she had been doing.

'Anyway,' Phil's voice was consoling, 'the two parts of the house are quite self-contained and, besides, he told me that he's come here to shut himself away for some peace and quiet, so I don't think you'll be bothered much by him.'

I wouldn't be too sure of that, Phil,

37

she thought grimly. Perhaps, after all, it would be best to look up Dawn and stay with her until he left.

'How long will he be there for? A couple of weeks?'

'Oh, no, I'm afraid not.' He shook his head regretfully. 'He took a long-term lease — three months.'

'Three *months*!'

'Yes — although he's already been here nearly a month.' He studied her face intently for a moment. 'Look, I'll run you out there — I think he could be a bit of a prickly customer if he chooses, and I don't imagine he'll be any more pleased to see you than you are to see him.'

Maggie was quite sure he wouldn't. She wavered for a moment. It would be reassuring to have Phil's sturdy frame alongside her at their next confrontation . . . But then she shook her head decisively. After that first encounter this was something that she had to handle for herself.

Outside, she stood on the steps of the

office for a few moments, then squared her shoulders resolutely and walked across to the hardware emporium opposite.

Twenty minutes later she had disentangled herself from the proprietor's wife, whose two daughters had been yet more schoolfriends, and emerged clutching a brown paper parcel which contained a large pair of wire-cutters . . .

* * *

She stopped the hire car, retrieved her cases from among the oleanders, then rolled on gently down the track to the gates. She got out, listened intently for a few moments, then caught up the chain between the opened cutters and, grunting with the effort, sliced her way through one of the links. Pulling the chain apart, she pushed both gates wide open, defiantly wedged them with the two stones and drove on in.

The sun was low, so that as she

approached the house was outlined against a molten-gold sky. Her stomach was doing a pit-a-pat of nervousness and, in spite of her determination to stay perfectly cool and composed, she found her foot going down just a little harder on the accelerator pedal. She scanned the veranda and lawns, but they were deserted. Perhaps he'd gone back to the beach for another dip, to cool off after their last meeting.

The gravel drive led past the length of the house then swept round to her parents' section at the rear, and she had already made up her mind to head straight round there, as though there was nothing out of the ordinary at all.

She was just passing the steps which led up to the house when the green mesh door opened and he appeared, cigarette in one hand, glass in the other. He was sauntering out, obviously very much at home, until he glanced up and met her gaze through the open car window.

He stood, transfixed, and afterwards,

when Maggie reviewed the events of that evening, she was quite positive that his jaw had dropped. Next moment, though, as he lunged towards her, she hastily averted her glance and the car leapt on round the corner.

He arrived just as she was dumping her first case near the side door which led to her parents' spacious apartment. The pitter-pattering inside her went into overdrive, but she pretended not to hear the rapid footsteps crunching over the gravel and bent forward into the car, struggling to remove the ignition key from the unfamiliar lock with a hand that was not quite steady.

'What the hell do you think you're doing?' He sounded ever so slightly out of breath.

'Unpacking.'

With deliberate nonchalance Maggie kept her back turned to him, kneeling up on the seat to fish out her second case.

'You know bloody well what I mean.' Exasperation and rage were fighting for supremacy in his voice. 'Just what do you think you're playing at? And how the hell did you get through the gates?'

'With these.'

She finally straightened up to face him, flourishing the wire-cutters within an inch of his nose. It was his turn now, she thought with a little spurt of satisfaction, to be momentarily bereft of speech. But then she saw the dark, angry flush on his cheekbones, his eyes, almost black in the twilight, sparking with fury, and the elation faded rapidly.

He was towering over her and, although he had put on a light blue T-shirt and white slacks, he still looked just as large and threateningly masculine. Perhaps it might be as well not to provoke him any more — in fact, it would be best to get safely inside the house, with the doors locked firmly against him.

'Would you excuse me, please?' she said, very politely, and picking up one case went to walk past him, but he seized hold of her arm, his fingers digging into the soft flesh.

'You listen to me. I don't know who you are, but you can just get the hell out of it. I don't allow pigheaded weirdos on my property.'

Pigheaded weirdo? *My* property? It was about time she put this hunk right on one or two matters. She wrenched her arm free from his grasp, seeing as she did so the bracelet of angry red marks. This *bullying* hunk, she amended silently.

'Now you can just listen to me for a change,' she said coldly. 'I tried to tell you earlier, but you wouldn't let me. This house — Moon Creek — is my home. My parents *own* this part — ' she gestured behind her ' — and I'm fully aware that you're here, as a *tenant*, in my grandmother's part of the house. I've come to stay — I have a perfect right to — and I intend to do just that.'

He eyed her in silence for several long moments, then, 'You know, I have an uneasy feeling that you just may be telling the truth.'

'Of course I'm telling the truth.' She swelled with indignation. 'But you can check with Phil Reid if you don't believe me.'

'Reid didn't tell me anything about this. I made it clear that I want absolute privacy.'

Absolute privacy? What was he, for heaven's sake? An invalid, recuperating from a long, desperate illness? He didn't look like one — and certainly didn't behave like one.

'Phil didn't know I was coming until a couple of days ago. But if it's complete peace and quiet you want — well, sorry, but you won't get it here.'

A sudden, wild hope was forming in her mind. If he was so obsessed with privacy, then maybe he would throw in the towel and move out to some even more secluded spot. If so, she'd be magnanimous about the rental. She'd tell Phil first thing tomorrow to return any payment he'd already made. They'd have no difficulty in finding other tenants — and far more agreeable ones, too. Well, they could hardly be less so.

He was watching her, eyes slightly narrowed, as though he too was doing some swift reassessing of the situation. Of course, her sudden appearance must have been rather a bombshell for the poor man. She put a more conciliatory tone into her voice.

'Phil said that you've got my house keys. Can I have them, please?'

'Really?' He raised his brows in polite enquiry. 'I don't recall seeing any spare house keys.'

So he was playing difficult, was he — happily leaving her to sleep rough tonight, in the car, or out here on the ground, with the local wildlife running all over her? So much for her sympathetic understanding.

'Oh, well, in that case . . . '

She walked past him and, dropping to her knees beside the door, scrabbled behind a clump of orange canna lilies. Oh, please let it still be here, she prayed silently, then her fingers closed on a

45

small plastic box. She straightened up and, opening it, drew out a key.

'So sorry to disappoint you.'

Smiling sweetly, she held it up for his inspection, then put it in the lock and opened the door. As she carried the first case inside, he shot her one look of thwarted anger then turned on his heel. Round two to me, she thought, as she fetched in the rest of her luggage and dumped it on the kitchen floor.

It was already dark indoors, but when she flicked the light switch nothing happened. Damn. She stood, frowning as she tried vainly to remember where the master switch to the apartment was. She'd have to get one of the servants to help her. They'd be in *his* part of the house, of course, but he couldn't object to that, surely.

Halfway along the rear veranda, she stopped. Just ahead, a slanting beam of light shone through the shutters of one of the long windows and she could hear his voice, raised in anger. Normally she would have withdrawn rather than eavesdrop, but tonight was different.

'Yes, Reid, well, maybe you didn't know she was coming.' So, he was on the telephone, with the unfortunate Phil on the receiving end. 'But I repeat, now that she's here, what do you intend doing about her?'

There was a long silence, and she edged forward cautiously a couple of feet until she just had his back in her line of vision through the half-open louvres. One finger was tapping an irritable tattoo on the small table beside him.

'But you knew the conditions when I took the place.' Another, briefer pause then a harsh laugh. 'Not realise she's in the house? Reid, do you *know* her, for heaven's sake? That one was born to be a pain in the backside, if ever I've met one.'

She levelled a baleful glare at his unconscious back but somehow stayed silent.

'So in that case I'm forced to rethink. I shall want to be out of here by the end of the week.'

Maggie, all but turning cartwheels of jubilation up and down the veranda, almost missed the next bit.

'Look out details of other lets for me, will you? I'll be in first thing in the morning. What? Yes, it is a pity. I've quite fallen for this place. Oh, and don't forget I must have a piano — preferably a grand.'

A piano? So that had been one of the attractions of Moon Creek, had it? Her grandmother's beautiful Steinway, crated like fine porcelain and brought out from England seventy years ago. She pursed her lips in puzzlement. Just who was this Steve Donellan? Oh, no — surely not another musician?

She heard the click as he replaced the receiver and tentatively cleared her throat. A moment later, he appeared at the terrace door.

'Well?'

'I — I was wondering.' She cursed the uncertainty in her voice. This was ridiculous — they were her servants far more than his. 'The power is off in the

48

apartment and I don't know where the switch is. If I could just get Adela or one of the others to put it on again.'

'No, you can't.' Before she could bridle up, he went on, 'They aren't here. I've sent them away.'

'You've sent them away?' Maggie's voice rose to an outraged squeak. 'Of all the — how dare you? Don't you realise that some of them have worked for us since — since — ' She broke off, almost weeping with rage now.

He regarded her unsmilingly. 'I didn't say I'd fired them — just given them all an extended vacation, on full pay of course. Reid has no objections — and neither have you, I trust.'

'Well, no,' she muttered, her mind struggling to come to terms with this latest torpedo that just seemed to have slipped her grandmother's mind.

'I need to be on my own,' he went on coolly, 'and that includes servants. Miss — Adela?' She nodded. 'She's helping out in her son's liquor store in town. The maid — Loretta — she's back with her mother up in the hills. And as for Joseph — well, I hope he's busy sitting with his feet up, as I told him to. Satisfied?'

'I suppose so,' she admitted grudgingly.

It had been pretty high-handed of him — no more than she'd have expected, of course — but he had at least been extremely generous in his pursuit of peace and quiet. Just one more reason why her arrival should have angered him so . . .

They stared at one another for a moment, then she said, 'Well, I'll go back, then. And I promise I won't disturb you again.'

She was on her hands and knees at one of the kitchen cupboards, fumbling in the blackness, her fingers clammy with the fear of what she might disturb, when suddenly a pair of strong hands were lifting her clear, and he dropped down to direct the beam of a powerful torch into the dark recess.

Next second a huge cockroach,

glistening in the yellow light, scuttled out and Maggie leapt back with a piercing shriek, so that he all but dropped the torch.

'What the — ?'

'Sorry.' She smiled in shamefaced apology. 'I'm terrified of roaches.'

He looked up at her, his dark eyes gleaming in the torchlight. 'Weren't you brought up out here?'

'Yes, I know. I should be used to them, but I've always loathed them. It's their whiskers, I think. Ugh!'

'Well, anyway, the switch isn't here.'

He stood up and ran the torchlight slowly along the walls, then disappeared into the tiled alcove where the brushes were kept. A few moments later she heard a grunt of satisfaction, followed by the click of a switch, and the kitchen light flickered, then came on. He reappeared and they both stood blinking in the sudden brightness.

'Well — thank you,' she said awkwardly, and then, as he still stood there, 'You've left your torch on.'

'What? Oh, thanks.'

He turned it off then looked around him, taking in the units, which were bare of any utensils or food.

'Have you got anything to eat?'

'Oh, yes — plenty, thanks.'

She indicated the table, where she had dropped the bag of goat-meat patties and the can of cola drink which she had picked up at the beach bar. He regarded them with a frown of distaste.

'I meant *real* food. Haven't you — ?'

'Oh, this will do me fine,' she broke in quickly, terrified that he was about to offer to let her share some of his. She'd been too worn out this afternoon to shop properly, but the last thing she wanted was to sponge off her grandmother's tenants, certainly not this one.

'Well, if you're sure.'

He took a step towards her and, for the first time, seemed to study her face intently, so that the reassuring half-smile which she'd forced to her lips faded. Why didn't he go? Her head was aching, a grey cloud of exhaustion was creeping over her, and she longed to eat then collapse, mind-blown, into bed.

Besides, he was standing very close to her and in the confined space he seemed even larger, even more intimidating than he'd done in the open air. His bulk filled the kitchen, his outline all at once ever so slightly hazy against the light.

'Are you all right?' he demanded sharply.

Actually, she wasn't, but with the last remnants of strength she clutched at the table edge and straightened her back. 'Perfectly, thank you. But I'll just eat then go to bed. I'm rather tired — a bit jet-lagged, I think.'

He nodded and at last turned to go.

'Look, I'm sorry.' Some strange inner compulsion made her all at once eager to hold him there just for a moment longer. 'About my turning up like this, I mean,' she added, when he looked at her uncomprehendingly.

'Oh.' He shrugged, then turned away again. 'It can't be helped. And in any case, I'll be out of here in a couple of days.'

4

And when she got there, the cupboard was bare.

Very bare. Maggie peered gloomily into the dry goods larder. Well, what else could she expect? With her parents not having been back for over two years, and now the servants away as well, it was obvious there wouldn't be any food in the house. A pity, though, when, for the first time in many weeks, after the soundest sleep she'd known for ages, she was feeling what was surely *real* hunger as opposed to mere chocolate-starvation.

Wait a minute, though. Tucked away at the back of the shelf there was a large jar of instant coffee. She'd at least be able to make herself a drink — no milk, of course, but black would do. She fell on it with a little whoop of rapture, but when she finally unscrewed the rusting top, the grains were congealed solidly together.

Really! If *he* hadn't been so obsessed with his stupid privacy, she could at least have got the basics for her breakfast from Adela before stocking up herself later that morning at one of the Chinese-run supermarkets in Charlotte. There was nothing for it; ravenous or not, she'd have to get dressed and drive in there now.

She took a step towards the kitchen door then stopped, a broad grin breaking over her face. What an idiot she was — or rather, it was those eight years in London that had conditioned her into thinking that all food came neatly packaged from a supermarket shelf. The garden . . . The bananas would be over now, of course, but there ought to be some sweet oranges still — and maybe the first of the mangoes from that number seven tree over by the orchard wall.

In the alcove beside the kitchen there were some old flip-flops. She slid her feet into a pair, opened the door which led outside, then paused, looking down at her short white cotton nightie. Maybe she ought to dress anyway, or at least put on her housecoat. But there was no sound. The enemy within was obviously still wrapped in the slumber of the righteous. Well, he was, after all, a stranger and didn't know any better whereas she, like all those fortunate enough to be raised in St Hilaire, knew that the most wonderful part of any day, cool and freshly scented, was over by eight in the morning.

Cautiously, she tiptoed along the side of the house, flitted round the corner and saw, too late, at the far end of the veranda complete with coffee-pot and cup, a table, and seated at it, Steve Donellan. Before she could take cover he had seen her.

'Hey. Come here.'

He beckoned a peremptory finger, but she hesitated then finally walked towards him. After all, her nightie, though short, was perfectly opaque

— less see-through than a flimsy beach dress would have been. Putting down his cup, he leaned back in the chair, surveying her in silence through a haze of cigarette smoke, until she wished desperately that she'd at least combed her sleep-rumpled hair.

'Where were you sneaking off to in such a hurry?'

'Down to the orchard, if you must know.'

She tried to infuse a haughty chill in her voice but instead only heard an infuriating huskiness. How maddeningly handsome he was — and, stripped to the waist, he revealed an alarmingly broad expanse of well-muscled chest and shoulders under the smooth satin gold of his skin . . .

She swallowed and hastily began doing mental gymnastics, reducing that face to a few swift strokes of charcoal across a page, that magnificent torso to a Leonardo-like anatomical study.

'I suppose you finished all those disgusting patties last night.'

'They were very good,' she said indignantly.

In fact, it was well known throughout the island that it was far better not to enquire as to precisely what went into the patties, but the finished product still managed to be very savoury.

She went to turn away, but the fragrant aroma of the strong island coffee was weaving itself around her nostrils, making her almost dizzy with desire and destroying all her resolutions about not begging any favours.

'Er — ' she began.

'Yes?' He raised one quizzical eyebrow.

'I was wondering if you'd let me have some of your coffee.' It came out all in a rush. 'I'll pay you back, of course, as soon as I — '

'Sure.' He pushed the pot towards her. 'Pull up a chair, while I fetch you a cup.'

'Oh, n-no,' she floundered. 'What I really meant was, take it back to my — '

'How about something to eat?'

'Well, I . . . ' She gave in. 'Yes, thank you.'

'Toast?'

'Please. Anything will do,' she added hopefully.

'Good grief. You don't mean to tell me that you're one of those rare women who actually eats a *real* breakfast?'

Any minute he'd be dishing out insults along the lines of, 'Well, I suppose I should have guessed from the size of you.'

'Yes I am, *actually*,' she said warningly.

'Hmm.' He gazed reflectively at the ample folds of her nightie, so that she shuffled her shoulders uncomfortably. 'Bacon and egg?'

'Oh, no, I really couldn't let you — '

'Please.' He held up his hand. 'A woman who eats in the morning is such a novelty, I really must see this.' He stared down at the cigarette, still smouldering in his fingers, then suddenly hurled it away over the veranda rail and stood up. 'Let's go.'

But Maggie stood, staring after him. That superb body, adorned only in old espadrilles and a pair of boxer shorts —

He swung round. 'Now what?'

'Oh, nothing.' She could hardly tell him that she was drooling over his physique, even if it was purely from an artistic point of view. 'I — I was just admiring your shorts.'

He looked down, grimacing at the violent pattern of stars and stripes. 'A present from one of my kid nephews. His patriotism is stronger than his taste in underwear, I fear.' His mouth quirked for a moment. 'Normally, I only wear them when I'm not expecting company.'

Maggie followed him into the huge kitchen, but then backed up against the corner unit, watching him covertly from under her lashes. He was very much at home, and it was a peculiar sensation for her to be on such familiar, yet at the same time with him here, such unfamiliar territory.

He must have sensed something of

her inner confusion, for as he turned from arranging bacon slices under the grill he glanced swiftly at her then pushed the toaster towards her.

'Come on. Make yourself useful.'

There was a wicker basket of oranges on the table. He halved some in neat, quick movements and tossed them into the juicer.

'Freshly picked this morning.'

So he too had discovered the delights of the orchard, after all. If she went there tomorrow morning, she'd have to dress with a little more decorum. He reached past her into a wall cupboard for glasses, and as he did so his bare arm brushed casually against hers, sending strange little prickles from the nerve-ends just under the skin deep into her body. Moving back hastily, she became very busy with the toast.

The whole scene, she thought suddenly, had a strange, surreal quality about it. Here she was, just in her nightie, in her grandmother's kitchen, with a big blond bear of a man in psychedelic boxer shorts, carefully breaking eggs into a basin like a thoroughly domesticated teddy bear, but who just hours before had been manhandling her with a thoroughness which had stopped only just short of cruelty.

At the memory, she glanced down at her wrist, seeing the ring of small dark shadows where his fingers had seized on her. She cradled it gently in her other hand and shivered. A big man like this could so easily have broken her arm — or any other part of her anatomy — with contemptuous ease.

She looked across at him through her untidy fringe and, as she caught his eye, he pulled a wry face.

'I'm sorry — about yesterday, I mean. Maybe I was a shade heavy-handed. Although,' he went on, with a flashing grin, 'I guess it was kind of funny, wasn't it, my giving you the bum's rush off your own property like that?'

She regarded him coolly. 'Was it?'

'Well, why didn't you tell me, for Pete's sake?'

'I tried to — remember?' she snapped, but then reminded herself hastily that he was providing her with an excellent breakfast — and as he was only going to be around for another day or so she could afford to be all gracious forgiveness. 'But anyway, I can see how it happened.'

'You picked a bad day, that's all. I'd had a hard time in New York, and besides, I wasn't quite my normal amiable self.' You can say that again, she thought sardonically. 'I've stopped smoking and it's pretty tough going.'

'But you've been smoking this morning — and last night.'

He scowled. 'That was an aberration, brought on by the stress of having to turn you out.'

'Oh, come on.' She could not resist it. 'You enjoyed every minute of it.'

'Yes, well, perhaps I did, at the time.' He gave a reminiscent smirk. 'But then the reaction set in. Anyway, apologies accepted on both sides, and cessation of hostilities, till I move out. OK?'

He held out his large hand to her and as she took it he smiled down at her. The effect was quite devastating: the corners of his eyes crinkled, and his face lit up with a wholly unexpected warmth. Maggie was almost too over-whelmed to smile back, then as her knees threatened to buckle under her she sagged down gently on to a kitchen stool beside her.

'No,' he commanded. 'We'll eat outside.' Piling the breakfast things on to a tray, he led the way out. 'Right. Give me a hand.'

Bewildered, Maggie lifted one end of the table and together they side-stepped along the veranda.

'OK. Hold it.' Pursing his lips, he studied the house wall intently. 'Now, this window is my dining-room. That one must be in your part. So, if you sit that side and I sit here, the table is in no man's land — the forty-ninth parallel.'

She watched in secret amusement as he fetched two chairs and positioned them with exact precision, then sat down and made a start on the bacon and eggs. She ate rather self-consciously at first, but with increasing avidity — she really was even hungrier than she'd thought. But then she glanced up and caught his eye, glinting with silent satisfaction, and looked away in confusion through the screen of trailing purple and blue bougainvillaea to where, just visible through the trees, she could see the river.

She followed it lovingly with her eye to where it widened to the mangrove-fringed creek that gave the house its name, and then, in her imagination, on past the thick belt of palm-trees to the small private beach, a sliver of pale talcum powder sand. Later today, she must go down there. Until she did so, she wouldn't believe that she was really here.

'Beautiful, isn't it?' His voice made her eyes jerk back to him. 'How could you ever have borne to leave it?'

She pulled a rueful face. 'Exactly what I'm asking myself.'

'Where have you been living lately?'

'London — for the past eight years.'

'And you've not been back in all that time?'

'Oh, yes, I came quite regularly at first, but this is my first trip for four years.'

'So long?'

'Well,' she said carefully, 'with my grandmother getting incurable travel-fever at the age of seventy, and my parents having to settle in the south of France because the climate out here didn't suit Dad, there seemed nothing to come for.'

Quite apart from the fact, of course, that when she'd brought David out four years ago it had been an unmitigated disaster. The family had not taken to him, to put it mildly — although they'd been super-polite to him. He hadn't known, of course, that they were only polite to those they disliked; they were rude to people they liked and down-right insulting to those they really cared for.

And, although she'd so much wanted him to love this beloved place, David just hadn't been happy here. The heat had been too much for him, but far worse than that, he'd found the vibrant colours, the exuberance of her friends — the sheer physical, *animal* vitality of the island overwhelming. Finally, she thought sadly, he'd been repelled by it all, and she'd persuaded herself that her future lay in London. But she couldn't tell this sardonic-eyed stranger anything of this, of course. So instead, she went on, 'But I'm not here on holiday now. I'm here to work.'

'What do you do?'

'I'm a painter.'

'Are you any good?'

His direct blue-black gaze was disconcerting, but she forced a casual shrug. 'I think so. I make a living, anyway.'

'What's your medium? Oils?'

'No, water-colours, these days. I'm working just now on a series of flower prints for a Bond Street gallery.' She pulled a face. 'That's why I've come out here, really — in a last-ditch attempt to meet their deadline.' *And to prove to myself that I still can paint — that David has not made me hung-up forever.*

Something of the paralysing terror which had gripped her for the last six weeks must have communicated itself to him. 'Last-ditch? Why the panic?'

'Oh, I've just hit a block, that's all.' She tried to sound casual, but he still looked altogether too interested, so she said quickly, 'What about you?'

'Me? I'm a composer.'

'Music, you mean?'

He nodded.

'Pop music?' She was quite impressed.

'Good lord, no.' He sounded outraged.

'Oh, sorry. Are you any good?' She shot him an impish smile but he was toying morosely with his knife.

'Not just now I'm not. These blocks seem to be catching.'

He reached abruptly for the jar of guava jam, just as she leaned forward to take a spoonful. Their fingers grazed against one another and they both jerked back.

'After you.' This time, he did not quite look at her.

'Thanks,' she mumbled, and to hide her sudden confusion said, 'A composer. How wrong can you be? Do you know, on the plane I'd got you down as a stockbroker.'

'Good grief.' He laughed out loud. 'Whatever gave you that idea?'

'Well, you were reading an article on Wall Street, and doing all those complicated calculations on that envelope.'

'Oh, those.' The remnants of the smile died all at once and his mouth tightened. 'No, I wasn't checking out the profits on my latest insider killing, I'm afraid. That was something quite different.' He stood up, cramming in the last mouthful of toast. 'Right. Time I was seeing what Reid's come up with.'

'Leave these.' Maggie gestured to the litter of dishes. 'I'll do them.'

He half turned then stopped, looking down at her. His eyes were bleak, but this time she had the feeling that his sudden change of mood was nothing to do with her.

'You'll be going into town yourself, won't you?' he said.

'Yes, but there's no hurry. I can go later,' she said hastily. She certainly didn't want him to think she was cadging a ride.

She began stacking the dirty plates but he put his hand on her arm, giving it a little shake to make her release her hold.

'No point in taking two cars. You can come with me. Yes,' as she tried to protest. 'Go and get ready.'

* * *

'Oops, sorry. We really must stop meeting like this.'

70

As, yet again, they bumped supermarket trolleys at the end of another aisle, Maggie gave him an overly bright grin as she sped past, but there was no response. In fact, all the way into town he'd been withdrawn, barely acknowledging her brittle attempts at conversation. He'd not even commented as the hired Ford had swept through the propped open gates at the end of the drive, although she'd been steeling herself for some caustic remark.

What a moody man he was, she'd thought, covertly studying his profile as he had concentrated on the bumpy road ahead. She'd always considered *she* was changeable — up in the clouds one minute, brooding in some dark pit the next — although, in her case, she had some excuse, of course, being a Gemini, but compared with his quicksilver volatility she seemed almost stable.

No doubt, like her, he suffered — and suffered was the word — from the Artistic Temperament. Just like David. It was different, of course: David was a performer, not a composer — a violinist with one of the leading London symphony orchestras — but he too had had his black moods. They both had . . . Maybe that had been their undoing, finally. Two mercurial temperaments, cooped up in that tiny flat — it had been as dangerous as penning together two unpredictable tigers.

There had been that time — her lips had twitched slightly at the memory — when he'd stormed into the flat after a particularly fraught rehearsal of a piece by that modern composer — what was his name? Barshinsky, or something? — flung his precious violin down with such violence that it had nearly broken in two, and yelled, 'Lord save me from living composers. And it's not even music — just tarted-up film scores. Give me good old Ludwig any day!'

Oh, David! His name had been enough to give a sharp tug at her heart-strings and, feeling her eyes fill with tears, she'd turned quickly to gaze out at the cane fields flashing past the side window . . .

She had expected to be dropped off at the supermarket, but instead he'd parked the car.

'Well, I have to eat too,' he'd pointed out. 'I'll just get enough to keep me going till I move out, then go and see Reid. Give him a bit longer to come up with something suitable.'

Once inside the air-conditioned store, though, she'd seized a trolley and had fled. She had no intention of going round elbow-to-elbow with him; she could imagine all too clearly the cold eye he'd cast over her purchases.

Even so, he managed to arrive at the check-out simultaneously, and stared down into her trolley with a pained expression.

'Something wrong?' she asked sweetly.

'Sugar-coated cereals . . . frozen meal-in-a-minute steaklets . . . three instant noodles . . . four instant soups . . . and *ten* chocolate bars.'

'Well, what about it? I need a lot of energy — I have a very low blood-sugar count,' she said grandly. She was never quite sure exactly what that meant, but a friend had told her that perhaps that was what she suffered from.

'Haven't you got any *real* food in among all that junk?'

'Yes, I have,' she retorted indignantly, putting a protective arm across her precious chocolate bars. 'I've got these chicken portions, and — and — well, at least I'm not a health food freak, like some people.'

She scowled into the Donellan trolley, which, apart from some rashers of lean bacon and a frozen chicken, was nauseatingly crammed with wholemeal bread, natural yogurts, olive oil, fresh fruit and vegetables.

'Hmm.' He was still gazing transfixed at hers. 'No wonder — ' He broke off.

'Yes?' she demanded belligerently.

'Oh, nothing. After you.' And he gave her trolley a shove in the direction of the check-out girl.

Outside in the car park Maggie, still smarting, opened the boot lid and unloaded her box of groceries into it. As he bent forward to slide his alongside, two packets of cigarettes fell from his shirt pocket. She pounced on them.

'He-*llo*. What have we here?'

'Give me those.' He snatched them off her and threw them on top of his purchases.

'Tch, tch. Naughty.' She waved an admonishing finger.

'I was doing just fine before you came on the scene. These are just to tide me over till I'm safely away from you. Now, get in.'

He parked in the square and glanced at her briefly. 'Are you going to wait here while I see Reid?'

'No, I want some things from the drugstore over there.'

She did not go straight away, though, but leaned against the car, idly watching him as he walked away across the dusty patch of grass which surrounded the ornamental fountain put up to mark Queen Victoria's

Diamond Jubilee.

That thick, shaggy hair, bleached by the sun, the broad back stretched under the navy blue sweatshirt, the strong thighs and hips, outlined tautly under the blue denim shorts . . . He moved with surprising grace for such a big, powerfully built man. Like a dancing bear, she thought with a little smile to herself, then was surprised by the sudden twinge, not exactly of pain, but of sadness. It was going to be very quiet at Moon Creek when he'd gone . . . Oh, come on. You came out here for peace and tranquillity, didn't you? Not only to finish your assignment but also to do that invisible mending job on your ego, and your heart — and peace and tranquillity are always going to be in short supply with him around.

She slowly straightened up and walked across to the chemist. At the entrance to the beauty products area, a full-length mirror had been cunningly placed and Maggie, her mind still on

Steve Donellan, almost walked into her reflection.

Oh, lord, what a mess. But somehow she forced down the instinctive reaction to flee back to the car and fall on a couple of consoling chocolate bars, and made herself study that grim-eyed reflection more closely. She'd deliberately chosen a loose-fitting yellow sundress, but even so . . . And her hair really needed attention. She'd neglected it shamefully the last few weeks and it was quite dull and unkempt.

Her face, a small pale oval, dark shadows brushed under the grey eyes as though with a piece of her own charcoal; the wide mouth, still taut from the weeks of strain and unhappiness. Once she'd got a tan, things might improve a little, but . . . Maggie, my girl, she said sternly to herself, this has gone on quite long enough.

Taking a wire basket, she began systematically preparing for a head-to-toe renovation job: shampoo, conditioner, mousse, face pack, bubble bath, body lotion, sun-tan cream — and, finally, a dozen slimming meals. It was a pity there'd be no one around to see the results of her all-out assault — she pulled herself up smartly. For goodness' sake, she was only doing it to boost her own self-esteem, wasn't she?

When she finally emerged, he was standing by the car, his arms folded. She wanted to saunter but found herself hurrying towards him, clutching her packages to her. 'Sorry.'

She was panting from the exertion, but he merely grunted and opened the door for her to slide in, then got in beside her.

'Well?' She gave him a faint smile. 'Where are you off to?'

'Nowhere.' He jabbed the key savagely into the ignition.

'What?'

He reversed out of the car park, almost grazing a passing donkey cart, then shot off down the road.

'There *is* nowhere,' he snarled. 'Reid's run all his properties through that fancy computer of his, and there's nothing. The only other property with a halfway decent piano is in down-town Port Charlotte, right next to the noisiest dive on the island.'

'B-but there must be.' She stared at him in growing alarm.

'Sorry to disappoint you, honey. I've even been round all the other estate agents — with him being a friend of yours, I half thought Reid might be playing silly-fool tricks to keep a tenant at Moon Creek.'

'Phil wouldn't do that.' She bristled indignantly. 'And anyway, he'd have no problem finding another tenant — and somebody a lot less demanding than you.'

'Maybe. But it doesn't alter the fact that I'm stuck with you for the next two months.'

'*You* stuck with me!' she exclaimed furiously. 'How about me being stuck with — with — ?'

'OK — so we're stuck with each other.'

He jerked viciously at the steering-wheel to swing past a lorry, laden to the gunwales with sugar-cane.

'But — couldn't you have your own piano sent down from the States?'

She was clutching at straws, she knew, but she had to try and fight down the horrible sick feeling of inevitability that was creeping over her. Earlier, she'd felt that twinge of sadness; now she was panic-stricken. Moon Creek might be spacious, but somehow it was just too small for her to share it with this over-lifesize man.

'No. By the time it was crated up and shipped here it would be too late. I've got a deadline to meet, too.'

'So, what are we going to do?'

'What do you think?' he demanded. 'You never seem short of ideas — for getting into the property, anyway.'

He did not look at her — fortunately, for he was doing a speed more suited to a race-track than the potholed coast road they were now following.

'Well, I suppose I could always go

and camp on the beach until you finish whatever masterpiece you're supposed to be creating. I'd hate to deprive the world of a work of genius.'

She had to shout to make herself heard, for the wind was whistling through the open window, whipping her hair round her head in a red-gold halo.

'That's just the sort of damn-fool suggestion I'd expect from you.'

'Can you think of a better one?' she yelled. 'I came here for peace and quiet too, remember. Do you think I want to share the house with a loud-mouthed, overbearing — ?'

'And do you think I want to live alongside a small, round ball of fire?'

Small, yes. Ball of fire, OK. Round — definitely not. She swung towards him, her eyes sparking with temper, but then, at the jolting memory of that chemist's candid mirror view of herself, all the fight went out of her. Her head drooped, her mouth quivered.

He swore violently, braked and pulled off on to the verge. Before she knew what was happening, he had turned to her and taken her in his arms. She struggled feebly, but he held her against him until she subsided.

'Oh, honey, I'm sorry,' he said into her hair. 'I'm an ill-tempered brute. Forgive me?'

'Mmm.' Maggie could only nod. She was far too busy thinking how incredibly good it felt being crushed against that hard bear's chest to formulate words.

'You are gorgeous. Do you know that?'

'No, I'm not. I'm f-fat,' she whispered. There — the awful word was out.

'No — no, you're not.' She felt him shake his head emphatically. 'You are the most completely feminine, most utterly cuddleable woman I have ever met.'

She murmured protestingly as he held her away from him by the elbows and looked down seriously at her. Oh, those blue-black eyes — you could let yourself fall into them, helplessly drowning.

'And that — plus the fact that I really do need to work — is precisely why it is *not* a good idea for us to stay under the same roof.' He gave her a slanting, rather wry smile. 'Cuddleable or not, I have no intention of getting mixed up with any woman.'

Maggie slowly subdued her twittering wits. 'That's fine by me.' She felt the pink creep into her cheeks but forced herself to hurry on. 'I've had more than enough of any — sentimental entanglements, believe me. The very last thing I'm looking for is anything of that sort.'

He studied her intently. 'Still hurts, does it?'

'Yes,' she said briefly, already regretting that she'd been tempted into giving even this much away.

He leaned forward, little by little, until she could feel his breath, warm on her cheek. Then, as she stared up at him, their eyes just inches apart, he gently dropped a kiss on her nose. He straightened and grinned at her, all ill humour seemingly forgotten.

'I've wanted to do that ever since we met. The most perfect snub nose I've ever seen.' He tapped it softly with the tip of his finger. 'Now, about our cohabitation. Can we manage it, do you think?'

Cohabitation? That wasn't the word she'd have chosen. Alarm bells rang in her mind, but she decided to let it pass. 'I'm very quiet,' she assured him solemnly.

'Really?' He laughed in open disbelief. 'But I suppose, if we each stay firmly in our own halves, and reach some agreement on the use of the grounds and the beach, we needn't know the other one is even there. So — is it a deal, Maggie?'

'A deal — Steve.' And her small hand was engulfed in his large one . . .

★ ★ ★

He pulled up outside her door. 'I'll carry your stuff in.'

84

'Oh, no, I can manage,' she protested.

But he insisted, taking her box into her kitchen and dumping it on the table, then he stood looking down at its contents.

'Really.' He shook his head sadly.

'I thought we weren't going to interfere with each other — and you know what I mean,' she added, as he flashed her a wicked grin.

'Yes, but even so. How I can possibly live under the same roof as a junk-food addict — ?'

'Will you just mind your own business?' she protested.

'Can't you cook?'

She shrugged. 'Life's too short to waste in the kitchen.'

'Am I hearing right?' He rolled his eyes, picked up the instant noodles and dropped them again in mock horror. 'Look — come round to my half tonight. I'll show you what a real dinner's like.'

'No, thank you.'

'Nothing too fancy. Just chicken Kiev, rice, green salad.'

Chicken Kiev. How did he know that it was one of her favourite meals?

'No,' she said, very firmly. 'Thanks, but I'd better not. We must start the way we mean to go on. Besides, it would be so easy . . . ' Her voice trailed away.

'So easy?' he prompted.

'Oh — so easy for a lazy slob like me to take advantage of living alongside a cordon bleu cook like you.'

He shrugged indifferently. 'OK, have it your own way. Enjoy your junk dinner.'

5

When Steve had gone, Maggie unpacked her groceries. The chocolate bars were already softening in the heat so she stacked them away in the bottom of the refrigerator, then straightened up, brushing damp strands of hair away from her face. She drew down the bamboo blinds to screen the room, poured herself a cold drink and sat at the kitchen table.

The door to the rest of her part of the house stood open, and, from beyond the flimsy board partitions which had divided Moon Creek since her parents' marriage, she could hear Steve Donellan moving about. The bump as he closed a door, the sound of running water echoing softly through the pipes just above her head, a creak of floorboards as he went upstairs . . . She found the noises disconcerting — almost disturbing — and tried, unsuccessfully, to close her mind to them.

Cuddleable . . . The most perfect snub nose I've ever seen . . . A few minutes ago, she'd been on the point of saying, 'It would be so easy to get fond of you,' and she mustn't do that. There was no way she was going to jump casually from the frying-pan straight into the fire. It was maybe just as well, though, that he seemed equally determined to avoid anything approaching a romantic involvement — 'I have no intention of getting mixed up with any woman' . . . Yes, he, too, must have got his fingers burnt somewhere along the line.

Through the open door she could just catch a glimpse of the sea between the trees. She'd go down to the beach — in fact, she'd spend the rest of the day there. Marvellous. She went to get up, but then dropped down again.

She *must* paint. That was why she was here — and the fact that the mere thought of picking up her brush sent eddies of panic rippling through her made it all the more imperative that she did so, *now*. If she wasn't careful, she was going to have all the numbing terror of a full-blown creative block on her hands.

She set her mouth in a determined line. No beach until she'd at least *tried* to get back into the painting — she'd stick to that, if it took her a month.

Gathering up her case with all her gear, she went along to the end of the passage where there was a small room. She opened the shutters and looked round it critically. Large table, stool — this was where she'd worked when she'd first started painting seriously while still at school. Some old junk in the corner, but she could clear that away. Big picture window for maximum light — facing inland, so she wouldn't be tempted by any views of beach or sea. Yes, this would be ideal.

She unpacked her case, fetched a jug of water and her small portable tape recorder. She slipped into her old paint-stained smock, inserted one of the pop tapes she always used when she was painting to free her mind of outside distractions, and, wrestling with those butterflies of fear that were fluttering around her stomach, she sat down.

Gradually, painfully gradually, she became engrossed in the notebook of working studies which she had made in London, and imperceptibly everything external slipped away from her in the effort of finding exactly the right shade to reproduce the white-just-touched-with-softest-cream of the Lady Alice Fitzwilliam rhododendron . . .

The door behind her flew open and Steve Donellan, clad only in a short black silk dressing-gown which left his legs and half his chest exposed to her stunned gaze, came bursting in. His face flushed, he advanced on her. 'Switch that bloody thing off, will you?'

Brutally ripped out of her intense concentration, she barely registered his words. Quickly averting her eyes, she said, 'I do wish you wouldn't go around half-naked all the time.'

'What?' He glanced down impatiently. 'Oh, I always work like this. But anyway, turn that appalling racket off.'

'I most certainly will not. I need it when I'm painting.'

'And how the hell do you expect me to compose with that mindless, moronic pap blaring out through the wall?'

'It is not blaring out — ' although she registered guiltily that little by little she must, without realising it, have been increasing the volume ' — and it is not moronic. They're my favourite group.'

'Yes, well, that figures,' he sneered.

She'd been about to apologise but now, almost equally enraged, she yelled, 'This is *my* part of the house, and I'll damn well play my tapes as loud as I please!'

She reached across and deliberately turned up the volume to maximum, until the noise was pounding off the walls. Next moment, with a furious obscenity, he snatched up the machine and hurled it out through the open window. In the sudden, deafening silence, Maggie heard it land on the grass with a sad little clunk.

'Oh!'

Beside herself now, she leapt up, caught her elbow against the water jug and sent it hurtling across her painting. 'Now look what you've done, you — you great oaf, you!' As she grabbed at the paper, it tore under her hands. 'It's *ruined*.'

She rounded on him, infuriated beyond all self-control, and landed a sharp, flat-handed smack across his face. His hands, fingers splayed, came up towards her and for a terrible moment she thought he was going to seize her and shake her like a rabbit, but then he thrust his fists fiercely into his pockets.

They stood, breathing hard and staring at each other across the fragile barrier of the table, then, tight-faced, he turned on his heel and went out, slamming the door behind him.

Leaning against the table for support, she stood straining her ears until she heard the silvery notes of the Steinway drifting in through the open window. It was the sound of someone struggling desperately to find the elusive phrase, the fleeting melody, but then, as she listened still, there was one angry, frustrated crash of discordant chords and silence.

With a long, shuddering sigh, she sank down on to her stool, gnawing her underlip and staring unseeingly at the opposite wall. She shouldn't have provoked him. Knowing all too well the mental pressures caused by a work block, she should have backed off. But that was her trouble, she thought sombrely. She never did back off. How were they ever going to work side by side — maybe for months? The very roof of Moon Creek would take off into orbit one day under the stress of the turbulence generated by the two of them.

She smiled faintly at her own image, then scrumpled up the ruined painting. It was no use trying to work now; her mood was shattered — like his, no doubt. She'd go down to the beach — after all, she'd kept her side of the bargain with herself. Methodically, she began gathering up her things.

★ ★ ★

Maggie had been half afraid that her memory had played her tricks, that this place was not as wonderful as she'd remembered. But it was. Soft, warm sand under her feet; overhead, the palms rustling their fronds; at the far end, Moon River, flowing gently through the mangroves to meet the sea, milky green and translucent at the shore-line, deepening to dark, opaque blue at the reef.

Her towel and beach bag fell from her hands almost unnoticed as she gazed, spellbound once more, then she peeled off her white cotton smock dress. The incipient bulges, top and bottom of her turquoise-green bikini, almost spoilt this perfect moment, but then, catching up her hair into a ponytail high on her head, she ran down the sand, splashing through the shallows and striking out to let the warm water caress and fondle her, until every jangled nerve and taut muscle relaxed.

When she finally emerged, she lay for a long time, her head cushioned on her hands as she stared up at the weaving pattern of dazzling light and intense shade above her. The last time she'd been here, David had been with her — in fact, on the few occasions she'd actually managed to lure him to the beach, he'd lain here, protesting that the sun had been much too hot.

David. Cautiously, she allowed the thought of him into her mind . . . It was strange, there was no pain now — perhaps finally he'd become only a pale, featureless memory, like a bruise which you had to keep pressing just to see if it ached at all. How right she'd been to come back; after just a day, Moon Creek was already weaving its magic around her. Unless it was

— horrified, she sat up, thrusting the treacherous thought from her, and reached for her smock dress.

She was almost back at the house when she heard the bellow of rage. Oh, no, what on earth was wrong now? She ran up the path and burst out on to the lawn at the side of the house, to see Donellan, still in his dressing-gown, racing across the grass in furious pursuit of a huge turkey-vulture.

She stared in astonishment; had the heat affected him, or their abortive row earlier? The bird was flapping its enormous black wings frantically but was still having problems with lift-off, and when she looked more closely she saw that it was clutching something in its claws. Then, just as its enraged pursuer closed on it, it finally became airborne and lurched up into a poinciana tree. Donellan snatched up a stick and hurled it ineffectually into the tree, but the vulture launched itself again and flew off unsteadily to join a branchful of its sinister friends, who had been watching the scene with great interest.

'This is all your fault.' As she approached him warily, he swung round on her. 'If you hadn't upset me, I'd have remembered it earlier.' When she looked blankly at him, he went on irritably, 'My chicken. I put it out in the sun to defrost and came back to find that mangy, scab-ridden — ' he seemed to be struggling for words ' — *turkey-vulture* making off with it.'

'Oh.' She hastily bit her lip to subdue the smile. Of course, he didn't know any better. No local would ever do such a stupid thing; there was far too much scavenging wildlife hanging around on the off-chance of a square meal.

He fixed her with a cold eye. 'Something amusing you?'

'No,' she said hurriedly. Then, 'I was just thinking that maybe they ought to be called chicken-vultures.'

He scowled morosely down at her, then all at once his lips twitched, he threw back his head and gave a great roar of laughter. 'Ah, well,' he said at last, 'after all my bragging, no chicken Kiev for me. In fact, not much of anything.' He pulled a face. 'I didn't want the hassle of clearing out a fridgeful of food when I moved.'

'Look.' Even as she spoke, she was regretting it. 'Come round to me instead. That is, if you don't object to a junk-food meal, of course.'

She smiled but he did not respond, only regarded her, frowning faintly, for so long that she put up a defensive hand to smooth her bedraggled hair.

At last he seemed to make up his mind and nodded brusquely. 'OK. Thanks.'

'Fine.' But that thread of tension still hung between them. 'Well — about seven-thirty, then.'

She went on in to rinse out her bikini and saw, sitting in the middle of the kitchen table, her tape recorder. Before setting off for the beach she had retrieved it from the garden, but it had not played and when she'd shaken it

98

there had been an ominous rattle. Now, though, when she switched it on, her pop music came booming out. He must have mended it — and picked that huge bunch of orange-flame tiger lilies in the jug beside it, as a peace-offering.

Rather thoughtfully, she went on through to survey the contents of her store cupboard. Instant soup, followed by instant noodles? That was what he was confidently expecting, wasn't he? On the other hand . . . Her eyes strayed to the shelf where some of her mother's cookbooks still stood. She pulled out a couple and began flicking through the well-thumbed pages.

Fifteen minutes later she sat back in triumph; yes, she'd cracked it. 'Enjoy your junk dinner.' She'd show him.

* * *

Maggie stood on her small patio, frowning down at the table. White cloth . . . pale green china . . . silver. What it needed was a finishing touch. She went back indoors, broke the long stems of the tiger lilies, divided the tawny flower-heads between two glass bowls, then put them on the table. The three small candle-lamps that she had lit earlier glowed, making a pretty shadow pattern of them on the cloth.

She had already dragged two bamboo chairs over from the old stable block and had arranged cushions in them; now she placed another candle-lamp on a small table between them. Beyond the coral and pink bougainvillaea that tumbled all over the airy wicker screen which partly enclosed this small, glowing oasis, there was the sound of the sea and the tropical whiteness of a full moon. Perfect. She gave a little smile of satisfaction.

But then, all at once, a little shiver of nervousness ran through her. To try and still the rapid, unsteady beating of her heart she moved round the table, fidgeting every piece of cutlery then moving it back to its exact original place. It was going to be a disaster

— she knew it. Why, oh, why had she invited him?

'I hope I'm not too early?'

Maggie jumped violently, dropped the fork she had been toying with and swung round. He was standing on the top step of the patio, a hard-edged, black outline against the soft paleness of the moonlit garden.

Her throat was too tight for speech and she could only stand watching as he moved forward into the circle of candle-light, her eyes taking in the short-sleeved navy shirt, which set off his light gold tan and straw-coloured hair, and the white cotton trousers that held his strong, firm thighs and hips in a loving embrace.

They stood regarding each other across the table. There was something in those dark blue eyes which made her even more nervous, and yet at the same time very glad that amid her frenzied activity in the kitchen she had taken time to shampoo and condition her hair, bath and, finally, put her feet up for ten minutes before putting on one of her favourite dresses — a loose, low-necked caftan in pretty cream voile — and piling her hair in a gleaming knot at her nape.

Endless heartbeats of time seemed to pass, then Maggie somehow pulled herself together, running her tongue round her dry lips. 'No, you're not — too early, I mean.'

'Good.' He too seemed to make a huge effort to shake himself free from whatever spell had been gripping him, and came forward. He held out a bottle of wine. 'I hope white is OK.'

'Oh, yes, fine.' Her voice still sounded slightly unnatural as she took the chilled bottle from him. 'Thank you. I forgot to get any this morning, and I can't find the key to Dad's cellar.'

'Shall I open it for you?'

'Yes, please. I usually manage to leave half the cork in.'

Her smile seemed to dissipate a little of the tension between them and he followed her into the kitchen, watching as she burrowed in a drawer for the corkscrew then reached down two long-stemmed glasses.

'Would you like to eat straight away?'

'Whenever you want.'

As she opened the fridge door to take out the two plates of avocado vinaigrette that she'd prepared, she saw the cache of chocolate bars and hastily closed it, but too late.

'So you've got some left, then?'

'I've only had two bars — so there.' Amazingly, that was true. She couldn't remember a day when she hadn't eaten at least five by now.

'You really shouldn't, you know. Why not let me look after them for you?' he said cajolingly.

'We-ell.' She cast an anguished glance at the fridge door then thought, Out of sight, out of mind. Maybe it's not such a bad idea . . . 'All right, then. But only if you let me have your cigarettes.'

'Oh, no. I don't need your help, thanks. I've got enough will-power of my own.'

'Yes, I've noticed,' she said drily.

'Like this morning, before breakfast, for instance.'

He rolled his eyes. 'But you don't know the strain I'm under.'

She gave a mirthless laugh. 'With a strict deadline for the gallery to meet and next to no inspiration, I think I just might.'

'OK, then,' he said reluctantly. 'My cigarettes for your chocolate.'

And, before she could protest that she hadn't meant *this* soon, he had scooped out her hoard, disappeared and had come back with a pack of twenty cigarettes, which he solemnly gave to her.

'And the other one.'

She held out her hand and he gave her a guilty little-boy-found-out look and slowly produced the second pack from his trouser pocket. She put them away in the wall cupboard and turned back to him with a meaning look.

'And don't come sneaking in here for them at three a.m.'

'All right — but you're welcome to

come sneaking into my half at three a.m. — not for chocolate, though.'

The little battle of wills had seemed to ease the tension between them, but now, even as he spoke, his lips tightened as though he was furious with himself. He snatched up the wine and glasses and disappeared out to the patio, leaving her to follow with the avocados.

★　★　★

The silence, apart from the scraping of spoons, had gone on for too long. Her eyes strayed to the table decoration.

'Thank you for the flowers — and for mending my tape recorder,' she murmured.

He grimaced. 'The least I could do.'

'I'll keep the volume down in future, I promise.'

'Oh, that reminds me.' He fished out an audio tape and slid it across to her. 'If you're looking for wallpaper music tomorrow, try this.'

She held the tape up to the light.

'Film scores by Barshinsky?' She pulled a face. 'Oh, I don't fancy that.'

'Why not?'

'Well . . .' She remembered David's tantrum after that fraught rehearsal. 'He's very avant-garde, isn't he? All clashing chords and jingle-jangle.'

'He is not.' He shot her a pained look. 'The trouble with you is that you're hooked on that pop garbage.'

She opened her mouth to come back at him but then closed it. She was the hostess tonight, she reminded herself sternly, and good hostesses did not pick fights with their guests, however provoking they might be.

'Well, surely taste in music is an individual thing?' she said carefully, and he grunted a grudging assent. 'Mind you,' she went on, 'you must admit he's very difficult. Even musicians find him hard going.'

'Hard going?' he exclaimed hotly. 'I think you'll find that depends on the musicians. I certainly don't make concessions to second-raters.'

'What did you say?' She stared at him, her wine glass suspended halfway to her lips.

'Oh, nothing.' His lips clamped together angrily, but too late to take back the words.

'You said, *I* don't believe in making concessions.'

'Well, what of it?'

She was still staring at him. 'Are — are you Stefan Barshinsky?'

He nodded reluctantly. 'Got it in one.'

'But what's all this Steve Donellan business, then?'

He laughed shortly. 'Well, let's just say that I'm Stefan Barshinsky to my adoring public, and Steve Donellan when I come to a Caribbean hideaway seeking peace and quiet — unsuccessfully, of course.' He gave her a meaning look. 'But it's no con. My full name is Stefan Donellan Barshinsky.'

'Phew, that's a bit of a mouthful.' Her first astonishment was fading slightly.

'Well, blame my grandparents. One

from Lithuania, one from Russia, two from Ireland — and they all met up in Boston.'

'Stefan Barshinsky,' she murmured absently, then smiled to herself. 'I remember David carrying on alarmingly about — '

'David? Who's David?'

Her turn now to regret her unwary tongue. 'Oh, a friend,' she said hastily. 'He's a violinist with the London — '

'He's the one, isn't he?'

She was about to deny it, but then said simply, 'Yes.'

He was watching her intently across the table, the candle flames flickering in his dark eyes. 'Do you want to talk about it?'

'I don't know,' she said slowly, but then heard herself say, 'Yes — but there's not much to say.' Her grey eyes were fixed on her plate. 'We met when we were students — he was at music college and I was at art school. We moved into a flat and stayed together — oh, nearly six years. Then — ' in spite of her self-control, her voice trembled slightly ' — a couple of months ago, he announced that he was getting married — to a merchant banker's daughter. I hadn't suspected a thing — didn't even know that he'd met her.' She paused. 'I don't blame him — at least, not now.' She gave a wry little smile. 'After all, being a musician is a precarious business, isn't it? One accident to his hand, and he's on the scrapheap.'

But he dismissed the possible dangers to David's career with a contemptuous gesture. 'And how did you take it?'

'Badly, I'm afraid.' She grimaced ruefully and briefly met his gaze, then her lashes fluttered down again, screening her eyes. 'In fact, it really knocked me sideways. I'd got so used to having him around, you see — and he was very good for me in lots of ways. I'm very moody — in case you haven't noticed — and, although he was temperamental himself, he usually managed to keep me on an even keel. And he was a great help with my painting, encouraged me to develop my own individual style — so I'll always be grateful to him for that.'

'Why didn't you marry him?'

'Oh, you know.' She shrugged faintly. 'We just didn't get round to it, somehow.'

'But you loved him?'

She stirred restlessly under his inexorable prodding, but then she said flatly, 'I don't know. I thought I did, but now I can't feel anything much at all.'

She looked up, half expecting to see in his eyes contempt for her weakness, but there was only compassion and, fleetingly, another expression, which made her stomach skid with alarm. With this man, at least you knew where you were when there was blazing anger in those navy eyes, or when he was hurling abuse — and tape recorders — around. But sympathy — or anything else — was altogether different, and something she wasn't at all sure she could handle.

'I — I'll fetch the next course.'

Precipitately, she leapt to her feet and almost ran from the terrace.

6

In the kitchen, though, her agitation subsided under the effort of serving up the meal elegantly, instead of throwing it on to the plates in her usual manner. When she went back outside, he was leaning against the wooden rail, apparently contemplating the night.

'Ready,' she said, and as he turned she set down the serving dish with a flourish. 'Chicken Kiev suit you?'

When she saw his face the triumphant laughter bubbled out of her, but next second it changed to a breathless squeak as he snatched her up in an exuberant bear-hug.

'You crafty little thing — you said you couldn't cook.'

They were looking into each other's laughter-filled eyes, but then he abruptly set her down again and took his seat. While she served, he refilled their glasses, then she watched anxiously as he sliced through the end of his chicken fillet to let the buttery-garlic juices come pouring out.

'This is really delicious.'

He only just managed to keep the astonishment out of his voice, and Maggie repressed a smug, clever-cat smile. No need to admit that she'd never made it before — only watched her mother, whose favourite party dish it was, prepare it so often that once she'd got over her terror this afternoon it had almost made itself.

* * *

'Mmm.' Reluctantly, Steve pushed his empty dish away. 'Do you know, that's the very first time I've eaten mango fool.'

'Well, actually,' Maggie's lips curved in a rueful smile, 'it was meant to be mango ice-cream, but it didn't have time to freeze.'

'No matter. It was superb — food for the gods.'

'Thank you,' she said modestly.

In fact, all she'd done was mash ripe mangoes, fold the deliciously scented pulp into whipped cream and hurl the lot into the freezer, but there was no need to tell him that, either.

'I'll have to return the compliment one evening.'

'That will be nice — just so long as you remember that you're not feeding the local turkey-vultures,' she added demurely.

He insisted on helping her carry the dishes through to the kitchen, then she brought out a tray of coffee and put it on the low table between the two bamboo chairs. They sat in companionable silence for a while and Maggie even began to let herself succumb to the relaxing drowsiness brought on by the three glasses of wine she had drunk.

It was Steve, leaning back in the shadows, who finally broke the silence. 'Have your family lived at Moon Creek for very long?'

'Oh, yes. They came out from

England originally in the eighteenth century. They used to live in Port Charlotte, but then my — I think it was my great-great-great-grandfather — freed his slaves early, before the Emancipation Act, and all the other plantation owners cold-shouldered him for that. So he bought land out here and built the house, and the family have lived here ever since.'

'They were in the sugar business?'

'Yes, but my grandfather sold most of the land — oh, about forty years ago.'

'What about your father?'

She took a sip of her coffee. 'Oh, Dad came out to work as an accountant with a shipping firm in Port Charlotte. That's how he met Mum. But the humidity never suited him and when he developed lung trouble a couple of years ago they moved to Monaco.'

'And you've stayed in London ever since — painting?'

'That's right,' she replied briefly. She was growing slightly uncomfortable under his cross-examination. 'More coffee?'

'Please.' He watched as she refilled his cup, then, just as she was setting it down, said casually, 'I'd like to see some of your paintings some time.'

Her wrist jerked, spilling a few drops of coffee into the saucer. 'Oh, I'm sorry.' She was aghast at the very idea of laying out any of her babies for his approval; if he didn't like them, that might set up her block all over again. 'Really, there's nothing to show you. What I was doing this afternoon, well, I screwed it up — literally, if you remember — and I haven't any of my other work with me.'

'OK.' He seemed to accept her rather brusque refusal. 'Maybe when you've finished them?'

'Perhaps,' she said non-committally, and bent forward to refill her own cup.

As she did so, she felt the pins that were holding that precarious knot of silky hair begin to slip. She set the coffee-pot down and started refastening it, but the next moment her hands were removed and with a deft flick he had released the remaining pins, so that her hair tumbled to her shoulders. Before she could move, he had captured a thick strand and held it up, to let it fan out through his fingers.

'Your hair is lovely, do you know that?' he said softly. 'So many colours — red, gold, auburn. And here's a blonde one.'

His face was very near hers, but after one sideways glance at his expression she kept her eyes averted.

'In fact,' he was almost musing to himself, 'your hair, your creamy skin, the way you hold yourself — you're just like one of those tiger lilies over there.' He laughed softly. 'Come to think of it, there's more than a touch of the tiger cub about this particular lily, I think.'

'But a very *round* one,' she murmured innocently, and his laugh stirred the tendrils of hair which screened her face.

'Now I thought we'd buried that particular hatchet. And anyway, you're looking slimmer already. It must be all those chocolates you're not eating.'

He was very near her, his voice husky in her ear. Even with her eyes averted, he somehow filled her line of vision; the sandalwood scent of his after-shave was in her nostrils, and beneath that, very faintly, the musky aroma of that powerful masculine body.

All at once, from the dark corners of the patio beyond the flickering candle-light, the tension began to stir and uncoil itself.

'And how about you?' she asked abruptly. 'What are you working on at the moment?'

He laughed ironically. 'What am I *supposed* to be working on, you mean? I've been hired to write the score for Konstantin Astrov's new movie.'

'Oh, of course, I'd forgotten. You've done other film scores for him, haven't you? That Mexican Civil War one with Jude Renton.' She looked across at him, wide-eyed. 'You won a special award at the Cannes Film Festival for that, didn't you — or was it an Oscar?'

He grimaced. 'Both, actually — but I'm not likely to win any doorsteps for this one, the way it's going — or rather, isn't going. I didn't really want to take it on. It's too much like the last one — another war epic. World War One, this time.'

'Why are you doing it, then?'

'Needs must, when the devil drives. I need the money.'

'That sounds very mercenary for a composer dedicated to his art.'

But he did not respond to her teasing tone. 'You'd be mercenary if you had an ex-wife determined to rip you off for every cent you possess. I've been up in New York, talking alimony with my lawyer — those 'complicated calculations' that you were so interested in on the plane, those were her latest terms.'

But she was barely listening. Ex-wife . . . So he'd been married — and, from the harshness that had entered his voice, the marriage had ended in bitterness and recrimination. Impulsively, she put her hand on his. 'Do you want to tell me about it?' she asked softly.

'Very little to tell. Nadia's a ballet dancer — we met when her company was performing a ballet choreographed to some of my music. We broke up a couple of years ago.'

'Why?' The question was blunt, but the need to know was driving her.

He shrugged morosely. 'Just general incompatibility. That, and the fact that she wouldn't have children. She was afraid they'd ruin her career.' He stared down at her hand for a moment, apparently realising for the first time that it lay on his, and drew back his own. 'I don't blame her for that — just that she didn't see fit to tell me before we were married. I come from a big family, you see, so I'd always dreamed of having lots of kids.'

'And how long were you married?'

'Ten years.'

Maggie felt the compassion welling in her heart. How he must have loved her, to hang on for that long. 'But since the divorce, why haven't you — ?' She paused delicately.

'Married again, you mean? I thought I would, but somehow Nadia seems to have managed to put me off the whole idea.' His mouth twisted into a harsh line. 'No, I reckon I've had more than my fill of marriage. I've come to the conclusion there's a great deal to be said for a musician — and certainly a Gemini musician — living alone.'

'You mean, you're a *Gemini*?' Maggie was horrified.

'That's right.' He reached into the open neck of his shirt and pulled out a chain with a roughly cut silver nugget hanging from it. When she peered at it she saw carved in relief the impression-istic representation of two embracing figures, one male, one female.

'I got it in Mexico. I had a couple of months there to soak up the atmosphere before I did that score.' But then he caught her expression. 'Oh, no, don't tell me — *you* as well?'

She nodded.

'I might have known. Restless, unpredictable, highly strung, emotional, changeable from minute to minute, full of complexities — have I got it about right?'

She pulled a face. 'You might have. If you knew how I used to long to be a calm, feet-on-the-ground Capricorn. But we Geminis can't help it, of course — it's just the stars we were born under.'

'Of course,' he agreed solemnly. 'But all the same, it's no wonder we can't cohabit amicably for more than an hour at a time.'

Maggie felt the blush zing into her cheeks. 'We do *not* cohabit.'

He gave her a slow, wicked smile. 'Well, we live under the same roof — and that partition's pretty flimsy, you know. I heard you taking a bath earlier, while I was shaving.'

The image which his words conjured up was somehow deeply disturbing. For an instant she stared at him, then began snatching the cups and saucers together, but he put a large hand on her wrist.

'Leave them. I'll help you later. It's such a lovely evening out there.' He gestured towards the garden. 'Let's take a walk.'

'Oh, but . . . '

She'd far rather have been left alone to vent her tangled emotions on the washing-up, but his hand was still on her wrist, and next moment, with no conscious volition of her own, she was out of the chair and down the patio steps.

The moon had gone behind a cloud and he was once again that intimidating black bulk beside her. Sliding her arm from his grip, she set off across the coarse grass, leaving him to follow. At the far edge of the lawn was a clump of small trees and she halted in the dense shade cast by their branches, drinking in the intoxicating perfume of their white, waxy flower-sprays until her senses reeled.

Behind her, there was a muffled

curse as Steve stumbled up against something. 'Maggie, where the devil are you?'

'Here — under the trees.'

She put out her hand and a moment later he gripped it hard.

'Whatever's this scent?' he asked.

'Frangipani,' she said dreamily. 'Isn't it wonderful?' His head was brushing the lowest branches, so that she felt a shower of small petals fall on their faces. 'In the old days it was a tradition for brides to wear a garland made from the blossoms. Gran's got an old brown photo of her mother — she was a Marguerite too — on her wedding day. It's really funny — she's sitting like a little ramrod in her whalebone stays and bustle and a white tulle hat, and perched round her neck is an enormous wreath. It looks — well — so incongruous.'

'Do they still do it?'

'Well, I think so, out in the country, anyway. It's supposed to bring — ' Too late, she stopped.

'Go on,' he prompted.

She forced herself to sound nonchalant. 'To bring fertility — and happiness in bed.'

'Oh, I see. One of those.'

She heard him laugh softly, then a moment later the snap as he reached up and broke off one of the twigs.

'Keep still,' he commanded, and before she could even tense under his touch she felt his warm fingers lifting her hair aside, then he gently tucked the sweetly scented spray behind her ear.

'L-let's go down to the creek.'

She was angry to hear her voice, breathless and uncertain, and she went to duck past him but he caught her hand again.

'I can't see a damn thing under these trees,' he said. 'I'll have to hang on to you.'

And Maggie, who could have found her way through the darkness like a cat, was forced to lead him through the low-hanging branches. It was all so strange, she thought involuntarily. The past years, she had so often dreamed of going down to Moon Creek on a night like this, and here she was — but with this man beside her, instead of David, his hand clamping hers, so tight that she could feel the pulse beat in his thumb, his trouser leg brushing against her bare calf . . .

Ahead of them a thousand fireflies were dancing, making little points of cold, green-gold fire, while in among the rushes an army of small frogs were croaking. As they reached the river bank, the moon slid from behind the cloud.

'This is Moon Creek.' In spite of her determination to appear casual, he caught the throb in her voice.

'You really love it, don't you?'

'Yes, I do.' Her breath caught in her throat as she realised for the first time exactly how much she'd missed this magical place. 'No one knows why it's called Moon River — although it's on all the old maps — but when I was a kid I believed that it was because in the moonlight the creek looks like a new moon. Look.'

She pointed to where the river widened out, just before it met the sea. The scrubby mangroves had melted away and the far bank was a perfect semi-circle of silver water, like the crescent of a new moon.

They followed the creek out to the beach, which still held the heat of the day, and stood side by side watching the pale points of moonlight play over the black waves, and the little patches of phosphorescence drifting just beneath their surface.

'Fancy a moonlight swim?'

'Oh, no.'

Maggie recoiled instantly. In fact, she loved swimming at night, turning on her back to paddle along, looking up at the sky, but for some reason which she did not quite understand she definitely did not want to swim tonight. In fact, she wanted to go back to the house — right now.

She half turned, but then stopped.

'That reminds me, though. We really ought to work out those lines of demarcation you were talking about. The house is divided, and so's the veranda — but what about the beach?'

'Oh, Maggie.' He laughed teasingly. 'Can't we share it? After all, it's big enough for two.'

No, it wasn't, not when one of them was Steve Donellan, or rather — she'd really have to get used to thinking of him as Stefan Barshinsky, although that somehow made him seem even more formidable.

'I'd rather split it, if you don't mind,' she said firmly. 'After all, we're both here to work and we'll do that much better alone.'

'OK, I guess you're right. Are you a morning or an afternoon person?'

She shrugged. 'Either. I work when I'm in the mood. Sometimes I get up at midnight if I've got something on my mind I want to try. What about you?'

'Well, *when* I work, I'm best in the mornings, but — '

'That's fine then,' she said briskly. 'I'll have the beach in the mornings, and you can have the afternoons.'

'But that still leaves the nights — especially the moonlit nights, doesn't it, Maggie?' His voice had developed a throaty purr. 'How do we split them, do you suggest? Or do we? Tonight, for instance — it's such a waste of a perfect evening.'

She hesitated; then, as her better judgement shrieked in her ear that she was a weak-willed fool, she said, 'All right. I'll go and get my swimsuit.'

'Oh, for heaven's sake,' he exclaimed. 'Of course, I wouldn't know what you're wearing under that delectable dress, but if the — er — garments are built on the same lines — '

'Don't you dare say it — '

' — as the ones you were flinging around at the airport yesterday, well, I'd say you were quite safe. But of course,' he shook his head in mock reproof, his teeth a white gleam against the dark shadows of his face, 'if you're *chicken* . . . '

That did it. 'Go down to that end of the beach — right down.' She pointed a dramatic finger.

'Yes, ma'am.' He tugged an obedient forelock.

'And stay there,' she called after him.

Once he was gone, lost in the shadows, she went down to the water's edge and stood for a few moments, the little wavelets licking warm tongues against her toes. Then she quickly pulled her dress over her head, took a swift glance at the reassuringly opaque white cotton of her bra and pants, then waded out and slid down into the water.

She swam for a while then turned on her back to float. The sky was an immense purple-black dome, speckled with a million stars; the land was dark, with an intense blackness which, living for eight years in a city, she'd forgotten existed. There was not even the orange glow from Charlotte Airport five miles along the coast — the last plane must have landed for the night. She could be quite alone on the planet.

But she wasn't alone. Somewhere along there, *he* was swimming. She turned over and trod water, peering through the darkness until her eyes ached, but there was no sign of him, no blond head bobbing through the waves. Perhaps she should have warned him not to go too near the mouth of the river, where there was always a slight undertow. She'd assumed he was a strong swimmer, but — oh, for goodness' sake, he'd swum further out, that was all.

But then, as she relaxed back into the water, she felt something brush gently against her leg. Shark? No, they never came in past the reef. Or did they? She sensed that faint movement again, opened her mouth to scream 'Steve' then, next second, a pair of large hands fastened around her waist.

With a strangled squeal, she twisted violently to escape but she was helpless in his grip, and a moment later he broke the surface beside her, shaking a shower of spray from his head.

'You said you'd stay down the other end,' she spluttered, flapping wildly to stay afloat.

'No, I didn't — *you* said I would. Sorry to frighten you — '

'You did *not* frighten me.'

' — but I got lonely without you.'

'Oh, you . . . '

Laughing in spite of herself at his pathetic expression, she reached out and grabbed hold of his shoulder, but before she could duck him he had twisted free like an eel and launched himself into a powerful crawl.

Treading water, she gazed after him, the moonlight glinting on his wake as he cleaved through the water. Those powerful arms . . . those muscled shoulders . . . At last he turned, but as he came more slowly back to her she was still watching him, quite unable to tear her eyes away. Too late, she realised that he too was watching her, intent, cat-like.

'What's the matter, Maggie?'

He must have sensed the hunger — no, the avidity in her eyes, so there was no point in denying it.

'If you must know,' she almost succeeded in sounding the cool, dispassionate artist, 'I was studying your physique. You really are a superb specimen. You could have modelled for that Greek statue — you know, Poseidon striding the waves. Tell me,' she was summoning all her aplomb, 'have you ever been painted?'

'No, I could never sit still long enough. But,' his eyes gleamed in the darkness, 'I wouldn't mind sitting for you. Would you like to paint me, Maggie?'

'Oh, no,' she said hurriedly. 'I haven't attempted the human body since life classes at college. I've done the odd portrait, but now I specialise in flower studies.'

'Ah, well, pity. Still, this superb specimen is here any time you want it,' he said, and she was certain that the ambivalence in his words was not accidental.

They were fencing with each other, she knew that, and to break the tension that was coiling itself round them again she looked up at the sky. 'What a glorious night,' she said huskily. 'All those stars — I suppose Gemini's up there somewhere.'

As if taking his cue from her, he too looked skyward. 'Oh, yes. Do you know how to find it?'

'No.'

'Come on, then. I'll show you.' And, seizing her hands, he towed her into the shallows.

'Now.' He turned her round, so that she was standing just in front of him. 'Look due north — no,' his laugh stirred the fine hair at her nape, 'that's due south.'

She felt him take hold of her head, fingers splayed, and gently tilt it. 'See those three stars in a row up there?'

She swallowed. 'Y-yes.' But she was far more conscious of that hard body against hers, so close that bare skin brushed bare skin, and the little droplets of water running down his flat stomach were trapped in the crevice between their flesh.

'Good. That's Orion's belt. Let your eyes go past them,' the hands were gently twisting her head, 'and you'll come to Gemini. It looks like a sort of cup on its side.'

'Oh, yes, I see it.' But the constellation was a reeling, shifting kaleidoscope which was making her dizzy, so that she had to lean against him to steady herself. 'Sorry.' Her voice sounded as though it came from a long way off. 'I lost my balance.'

'That's OK.' One hand came round her, to hold her to him, so that now she could feel his deep, regular breathing against her shoulder-blade. 'Well, at the base of the cup are two very bright stars. They're Castor and Pollux, the heavenly twins — our stars.'

Maggie stared up at them. Of course, it couldn't really be true that those two silver-blue specks, millions of light years away, could influence their moods, their personalities — their lives . . . could it? All at once, she shivered.

'You're cold.'

'No, I — well, yes I am.' Talking was still causing problems for her. 'I think I'll go in now.'

As she waded towards the beach, though, she glanced back at him. He must have swum through some of the phosphorescence, for he was gleaming softly as though that satin skin had been dipped in silver paint. Her eyes travelled slowly down to where his dark briefs clung wetly to him, moulding themselves to the strong masculine curve of his haunches.

Hastily she looked down at herself, and a faint gasp of shock was forced from her. The safe opaqueness of her bra and pants was lost, the white cotton moulded perfectly to her body too, revealing the full feminine curve of her breasts, the areolae dusky against her creamy skin. She flung both arms across her breasts in the timeless gesture of modesty, but then, glancing down at her pants, she saw the shadowy semi-circle of fine hair now all too visible.

Horrified, she turned blindly to make her escape into the safety of the night, but then stumbled and fell headlong in the water. She lay for a moment, helpless, then felt his hands round her, lifting her up into his arms.

'All right?'

He was laughing down at her, but then the laughter faded abruptly. He stared, frowning with puzzlement, as though seeing her for the very first time, and yet with the shock of recognition, as if he had known her a very long time ago.

'Maggie?' His voice trembled slightly.

'Y-yes?' she whispered, then her lips parted as, very slowly, his mouth came down on hers.

It was a gentle kiss, full of a sweetness which made her ache softly inside. When he raised his head, they stared at each other, their eyes blank with shock, then, 'Oh, baby,' he murmured, and bent towards her again.

This time, the kiss was not gentle. He thrust his tongue between her lips, demanding entry to the honey of her mouth until she drank the salt taste of him. All the feelings of her body were centred on her mouth; a violent shudder ran through her, and she put her arms round his neck, running her fingers wildly through his thick hair, clutching on it.

Without releasing her lips, he set her on her feet, sliding her down his body, so that she felt the sudden heat emanating from his damp skin, the pulsing of his desire. She sagged against him like a boneless rag doll and heard someone — herself? — give a tiny moan of surrender.

He strained her to him, so close that their few scraps of clothing seemed to melt away in the heat of their bodies. As they sank to their knees in a slow, endless movement, the water lapping round them, she ran her hands over him — that wonderful body that she had so longed to touch, the skin smooth as silk, beneath it the ripple of powerful muscles, and their play against bone and ligament.

He was sliding his lips down the line of her throat, setting off a trail of sparking electric current. Her fingers tightened on his shoulders and he gave a throaty gasp, then next moment she felt him tug roughly at the catch of her bra. Supporting her with one hand, he cradled her bare breast with the other as his mouth slid over the mound of wet flesh, to fasten greedily on her nipple, teasing it with his teeth and tongue until she felt it throb painfully with a passion that leapt to meet his.

She had never in all her life felt like this; she was drowning, helpless in the tumult of her own desire. But she didn't want to feel like this, she mustn't. At the very moment when she was being finally swept away, beyond reach of any saving reason, something — her instinct for self-preservation — flared into panic in her mind.

'No — no, Steve!'

She was pushing at his chest, frantically trying to free herself. For several moments he held her to him without moving, but then at last his harsh breathing steadied and she felt the tension drain from him.

'I'm s-sorry. I shouldn't have let — ' She broke off, biting her lip fiercely, as she battled with the sobs that were struggling for release.

'No, it was my fault,' he said tautly.

He was watching her, his face a sombre mask, and when she wriggled free from his arms he made no attempt to detain her, only steadied her as she almost stumbled again. Then he released her once more, to splash out through the shallows to the shore.

7

Steve caught Maggie up as she reached the house.

'I'll give you a hand with the dishes.'

'Oh, no, it's all right. I can manage on my own, thanks.'

She could not quite look at him but then, as he went to follow her up the steps, she said, '*Please*, I'd rather.'

Something in the softly spoken words must have got through to him. She sensed him regarding her lowered head for a few seconds, then he said brusquely, 'OK — thanks for a lovely meal.' And out of the corner of her eye she saw him walk away.

Somehow, she forced herself to clear the dishes, mechanically stacking them on the sink unit, then washed up, trying to fill her whole mind with the mundane task. As she bent over the sink, though, a single white frangipani flower fell from her hair and for several seconds she stood, gazing down at it, as it floated in the water, before snatching it out and throwing it into the bin.

Once in bed, she lay, staring at the thin needle-points of moonlight which filtered through the wooden louvres. How could she have done it? She almost writhed on the bed in anguished shame. How could she have let herself leap into his arms with such eagerness? Had it been the wine, the scented magic of a tropical night? No, she castigated herself savagely, that eagerness had not been the result of three glasses of wine; it had been desire — sheer, naked sexual desire. It had been as though he had put a match to her, and she had burst into instant flame.

With a groan, she rolled over and buried her burning face in the pillow. Never in all her life had she felt like this; not for one moment had David's lovemaking roused her to such heights — or depths — of passion, or made her feel so helpless, caught in the grip of terrifying emotions which she scarcely understood. Even now, something of those emotions remained so that her body trembled for his touch, ached to feel him take her in his arms again . . .

Maybe she should leave Moon Creek, after all. Perhaps it was just too dangerous to stay. She'd been able to stand up against his anger and his bullying, but could she resist other, more insidious threats? His physical manhandling had given her a few bruises, but bruises faded. She knew, with a flicker of fear, that they were nothing beside the lasting harm he could inflict on her.

The one thing she was certain of was that she could not allow herself to get involved in another affair. She'd never been wholly at ease in the relationship with David — it had been he who had resisted the commitment of marriage, arguing that a musician needed complete freedom to fulfil his art. And yet here she was, on the brink of an affair with another musician — this time a man who, for very good reasons of his own, was going to be even more unwilling to make any commitment whatever.

In the morning though, as, still undecided, she toyed with a slice of toast, she heard the sound of the piano grimly thrashing out variations on one World War One march after another. She listened, then smiled faintly to herself.

Consciously or unconsciously, he was showing her the way. She didn't want to leave Moon Creek — only now did she realise how much she didn't want to leave. She'd come here to work; he was here to work, and there was still no logical reason why they shouldn't, nor why that scene between them on the beach shouldn't be buried forever by the tide. After all, he probably regretted it at least as much as she did. They'd already agreed their pattern of separate existences and if she made it clear that, from now on, she was going to keep strictly to it, then surely so would he . . .

* * *

And that, Maggie thought with satisfaction, was exactly how it had worked out. For a week now, she'd barely set eyes on him, and when they did meet he'd been extremely correct but cool to the point of coldness and obviously in a great hurry to get back to his work. The work, though, seemed to be a different matter, with nearly every session ending with the crashing of chords and the slamming of doors.

Her painting was making better progress — at the rate she was going, she really might make that deadline, after all. But even so, despite the fact that the flower studies seemed to be at least as good as ever, she sometimes caught herself frowning at them with vague dissatisfaction. That camellia japonica she'd finished yesterday, for instance — there was definitely something lacking in it. And yet, what?

She rolled over on to her stomach and caught up a handful of fine sand, trickling it abstractedly through her fingers. Oh, well, she hadn't been able to see what was wrong with it, so hopefully nobody else would, either. Still, when she went back up to the house at lunchtime she'd have another look at it.

Reaching across to her beach bag, she fished out her watch and squinted at it. Good. Another hour, at least, before she'd have to leave — although, as usual, she'd have to make very sure that she was well clear before her time was up. So far, Steve had kept strictly to his side of the arrangement, not going down to the beach until well into the afternoon, and so she had felt quite safe in sunbathing nude — even, on several occasions, swimming naked, luxuriating in the silken touch of the water against her bare skin.

Still, she thought, suppressing a little

yawn, she had to make very sure she was gone before twelve . . .

★ ★ ★

A fly buzzed at her ear and Maggie rolled on to her side, to be brought up hard against something which rustled as she touched it and scratched her bare arm. Her eyes flew open and for a moment she lay staring up, quite disorientated. Just above her head was a lattice-work, black against the sky, with the sun filtering through the — what were they? Yes, palm fronds — in diamond chinks of light.

She must have nodded off, and while she was dozing *someone* had gathered up all the fallen fronds he could lay his stupid hands on and stuck them in the sand all round her like a tent. That just would be his idea of a joke, to come sneaking up on her — she sat bolt upright, then, catching sight of the expanse of tanned flesh, flung herself back down on the sand again. If it was

147

him — and really it couldn't possibly be anyone else — then he must have seen her.

With shaking hands, she parted the fronds and peered out. Sure enough, there he was, at the far end of the beach, stretched out at his ease in the shade of a palm-tree. How dared he? How could he? Burning with mingled anger and shame, she reached for her bikini, wriggled into it under cover of the leaves then stood up, kicking them aside before pulling on her pale green sundress. With two fierce swings of her beach bag, she demolished the remaining fronds then strode off across the hot sand.

He was studying a music manuscript book, but as she stood over him he put it aside and glanced up. 'Hi, Maggie. Come to take up my offer to let you paint me?' His lazy drawl inflamed her temper further.

'No, I haven't. How — how dare you?'

'Oh, sorry.' He looked pained. 'I

thought you were anxious to get me down in oils for posterity.'

'No, I'm not, damn you.' She hurled down her bag, half of its contents spilling on to the sand. 'You know perfectly well what I mean.' In spite of herself, a slow blush crawled over her cheeks. 'If — if you were a gentle-man — '

'Oh, not that again.' He rolled his eyes. 'Any minute now you'll be calling me a — what was it? — oh, yes, a cad.'

'And so you are. We had a *gentle-man's* agreement, but could you keep to it? No, you — '

'Now, just hold on a minute — ' His mouth had tightened angrily, but she swept on.

' — had to break it, didn't you?' Her voice rose shrilly. 'You've ruined every-thing. I'll never come down here again — you realise that?'

He scowled. 'Oh, don't be such a melodramatic little idiot — although, if my memory serves me right,' he allowed his gaze to wander over her body in a deliberately provocative gesture so that she was glad that she'd at least paused long enough to pull on her dress, '*little* isn't quite the word I'd choose to describe those delectable curves.'

'You — you — ' she choked.

'Anyway,' deliberately turning his back on her, he picked up his book, 'do me a favour, will you, and just go away?'

She stared down at the back of that blond head. Her foot itched to scuff into the sand, but some instinct for self-preservation held her in check. This was no seven-stone weakling, and she quailed inwardly at the thought of his reaction if she dared to kick sand all over him.

How she wished that she'd just gone quietly back to the house — and yet, why should she? He was completely in the wrong again, wasn't he? So —

'I'm afraid I shall have to reconsider our entire agreement.'

Steve muttered something she did

not quite catch, then slammed down his book. 'Stop behaving like a spoilt three-year-old, will you?'

That did it. The fact that she knew that she *was* behaving like a spoilt three-year-old only sprinkled salt on the umbrage. 'I don't need you to tell me how to behave.'

She reached for her bag, intending belatedly to make a dignified exit, but as she straightened up her temper flared again and she delivered a parting kick at his book, sending it spinning across the sand.

Next moment, Steve had leapt to his feet and snatched her up, tucking her under one arm as gracefully as though she were a sack of coal and striding away down the beach towards the sea.

'Put me down, will you?' she shrieked, with the little breath he had left her.

He paused on the very edge of the water. 'Going to apologise for being a shrew?'

'No, I won't. And if — '

151

But her threats were drowned as he splashed out through the shallows. He swung her up high into his arms then hurled her as far out as he could. When she at last rose, water streaming from her hair, her eyes, her clothes, he stood regarding her, hands on hips.

'And next time you come bawling me out, check your watch, honey. *You're* trespassing.'

'W-what?'

'For your information, it's two-thirty p.m. I don't know whether you were intending to spend the entire afternoon stretched out in the sun like that, but if so, you'd have been fried sunny side up by now.'

And, turning on his heel, he strode out of the water. She watched from under her dripping fringe until he reached the tree, retrieved his book and dropped on to his stomach, all without a backward glance at her.

In subdued silence, she waded out, her dress clinging horribly to her all over, flapping round her legs. For a few moments she stood, chewing her lip, then picked up her bag from where she had finally let go of it just before reaching the water's edge and stalked off across the beach in the opposite direction.

As she reached the trees, she paused irresolutely. She was in the wrong, of course. What an idiot she'd been. If only she'd taken the trouble to look at her watch — but then, that was her, wasn't it? Where angels feared to tread, there went Maggie Sanderson — leaping into battle like a pocket-sized Valkyrie. She really ought to apologise — but when she looked back in his direction he half raised his hand in an ironic gesture of farewell, so instead she tossed back her wet hair and set off for the house.

By the time she got there, though, her lips were twitching, and by the time she had rinsed out her clothes and spread them on the patio rail to dry, she was giggling so much that she had to sit down. She really had been very stupid, although — that slow blush began to spread through her again — it was quite understandable if she had gone over the top. But she couldn't bear him to think she was mean-spirited. Yes, she'd swallow her pride, go back down to the beach and apologise.

First, though, she went upstairs and combed her hair, now almost dry, into some sort of order, changed into a white T-shirt and blue and white striped shorts, then stood surveying herself in the wardrobe mirror. For the first time in weeks, she realised, she could actually do that without feeling totally submerged in depression — those surplus areas of flesh really were beginning to roll off her.

Since that very first day, she'd miraculously lost all taste for overeating, and for all the fattening things she'd seemed to need so badly. She hadn't used those slimming meals she'd bought — or even been tempted to creep into Steve's part of the house while he had been safely out of the way and go prospecting for those chocolate bars.

It was nothing more than the heat, of course — that, and the fact that she actually was making progress with her paintings — for, after all, fruit and salads were the sensible things to eat out here. But it wasn't just her weight; there was something else. She pursed her lips critically. Her skin was looking better, her hair too, and there was a kind of glow about her which had been missing for months. How right she'd been to come back to Moon Creek. It was exactly what she'd needed, even if she was having to share it with —

With a jolt, she remembered why she had come up to change, and went pattering off down the stairs and headed back to the beach.

He did not move as she approached and when, not without a twinge of nervousness, she came right up to him he still did not stir. He couldn't be — but he was — fast asleep, one arm resting on his book and his cheek pillowed comfortably on it.

She cleared her throat, but he did not wake. He really was sound out. Of course, she remembered now that several times the previous night she'd roused briefly and heard the sounds of the piano drifting through to her so that in the end she'd had to put her head under the pillow.

She stood looking down at him, seeing, with a funny little twist of the heart, the long lashes lying across the hard-planed cheek, the mouth, so often taut and strained, relaxed into softness. A stray lock of hair had fallen across his forehead and she found herself longing to brush it back. But she mustn't. Instead, she stood a little longer, allowing her gaze to wander down over that superb body, now relaxed totally, like a sleeping lion, and then, feeling guilty, as though she were intruding on his privacy, she turned away.

But then she stopped dead, as a lightning thought went through her. Dared she? He had told her she could, any time, hadn't he? But he was so unpredictable, how would he react? She stood a moment longer, tapping her foot indecisively, but then a slow, wicked smile spread across her face. She turned, tiptoed away and went flying back to the house to gather up her painting gear.

* * *

It was late afternoon when, taking in her dried clothes, she saw him coming up from the beach. Clutching the dress to her as a shield, she waited, her heart see-sawing wildly.

He came right up to her and stood surveying her in silence, then shook his head in exasperation. 'Can't you stay away from me?'

Actually, no, I can't, she thought suddenly, with a twinge of real fear. I can't stay away from you.

'Just keep off my back, will you?'

She was going to have to brazen it out — anything to hide the conflicting emotions he was rousing in her. 'Oh, but I thought it would be your *front* you'd be worried about,' she said innocently.

'You know damn well what I mean, you — you little paintbrush-wielding cretin, you.' With a dramatic gesture, he flung open his shirt. 'Just look at me.'

She studied his chest appraisingly. It was pretty good really, considering that as she'd crouched beside him on the sand, torn between elated laughter and mortal terror, her heart had been in her mouth all the time she had been working in case she'd woken the sleeping lion. But in fact, right to the end, he'd hardly twitched a muscle.

'Hmm,' she said at last, 'not bad — bearing in mind I haven't used acrylic paints for years, and considering,' her voice shook slightly, 'I've never painted a real fire-breathing dragon before.' She narrowed her eyes, as though in critical assessment. 'Of course, the tail isn't quite right. I wanted to continue it round your back but you wouldn't move. And that front paw is crooked. If I could have one more session — '

'Don't you come near me — keep away,' he exclaimed as she put her hand up to him. 'I'll go and get this mess off.'

'Without really seeing it?' She felt quite wounded. 'You must look at yourself first, Steve.'

'Well, all right,' he conceded ungraciously. 'Have you got a full-length mirror in here?' And before she could stop him, he strode past her into the house.

'No, not in there — ' she began, but he had already pushed open the dining-room door and was examining himself in the huge gilt mirror above the sideboard.

'Mmm — it *is* good, I'll grant you that — very realistic. You should set yourself up as a sailors' tattoo artist in downtown Port Charlotte. Mind you, a fire-breathing dragon isn't really appropriate for an easy-going guy like me.'

'Really?' she asked demurely.

'Yes, really. It's only cohabiting with a miniature fire cracker that seems to have changed my personality for the worse.' He took a last admiring glance at his reflection. 'Seems almost a pity to get rid of it, though.'

'It'll come off in the shower.'

'Yes, well, maybe I ought to take you in with me — make you scrub it off for me. Although, on second thoughts,' he added swiftly, as he caught the horrified look in her eyes, 'maybe not. Anyway, I guess I asked for it, dunking you like that.'

'No, I was wrong, flying off the handle the way I did. You saved me from a nasty case of sunburn, I'm sure. It was just — well, you seeing me — you know.' Her cheeks were reddening again at the memory. 'But don't worry — I'll make certain it doesn't happen again.'

'Oh, yes, I'm sure you will. No doubt Cinderella will be well clear of the beach before the clock strikes twelve from now on.'

160

'Yes,' she laughed, 'I'd hate to be turned into a pumpkin.'

'That was the coach, I think — and anyway, you're getting less pumpkin-like every day, you know that?' All at once, the laughter faded from his eyes. 'Maggie,' he began huskily, but then, as she stared at him, his lips tightened on whatever it was he had been about to say.

Abruptly, he swung round to leave, but then his eye fell on the polished mahogany table which ran half the length of the room. 'What are these?'

'Oh, just some rough sketches,' she said hastily, but when he looked at her in patent disbelief she went on reluctantly, 'They're my paintings for the gallery.'

'You've finished them? Great.'

'Well, I've got two more to complete, but then I'll be able to send them off. I — I don't like anyone seeing them before they're ready,' she added pointedly.

But, ignoring the hint, he walked over

and began studying them. She leaned up against the wall, covertly watching him as he moved slowly down the table, examining one after another of the paintings. Not by one tiny flicker of his face did he give away any impression of his thoughts. Occasionally, he picked up a painting for closer inspection, then each time set it down, with only the barest grunt.

Maggie's feathers began to feel ever so slightly ruffled. Of course, she hadn't expected him to break into cries of unrestrained rapture, but even so — well, she certainly wasn't going to demean herself to ask for his opinion. She'd rather cut her tongue out.

'Well, what do you think of them?' she heard herself say, as he straightened up finally.

'Oh,' he shrugged non-committally, 'I'm sure they're very good — excellent examples of their kind.'

The sting in the tail, she thought angrily. Of all the lukewarm . . . She'd far rather have had an outright attack on them.

'Of course — ' he began, then stopped.

'Oh, go on, please. Don't pull your punches on *my* account.'

She walked to the table and they stood facing one another across it.

He drew a deep breath. 'OK, then. They're pallid, anaemic. There's no heart in them, no soul — they're beautifully executed, joyless little pieces of work, by someone who ought to be darn well ashamed of herself.'

'Oh.' Maggie shot him a sizzling look. 'Well, thank you. It's just a good thing other people don't agree with you, isn't it? They happen to be *extremely* popular.'

'I'm quite sure they are.'

'I suppose I asked for it, actually inviting your opinion. I — ' her mouth quivered for an instant ' — I dared to say I didn't like your music, so I've just given you the chance to get even.'

His lips tautened into a thin line and he came round the table to her. For one terrifying moment she thought he was going to hit her, but he merely seized her by the shoulders.

'That has nothing whatever to do with it, and you know it.'

'Yes, I'm sorry,' she muttered, her gaze fixed on the floor. Why on earth had she said that? Whatever else he might be, there wasn't an ounce of petty vindictiveness or malice in the man.

Her eyes filled with tears suddenly, and she had to blink them away. She'd had criticism before — some of it, from her teachers, painful and personal in the extreme — but never had she felt so wounded, so that she wanted to crawl away into a hole and hide. Until he'd attacked the pictures, she hadn't realised just how desperately she'd wanted him to like them.

'I suppose you think I only ought to paint dragons. Is that what it is?' She gave him a rather blurred smile and his fingers tightened painfully on her shoulders.

'Oh, honey,' he began, but then he swung her round abruptly and marched her over to the window. 'Now, look out there — look around you, girl.'

In total bewilderment, she obeyed. There was the front terrace, with the purple and peach bougainvillaea sprawling all over it, that morning-glory vine, covered with huge mauve and pink trumpets, the abutilon, its scarlet flowers drawn back to reveal the gold stamens. A tiny, iridescent blue humming-bird was flinging itself rapturously into one golden heart after another, sending the nectar dripping in slow fat globules to the tiled floor . . . Beyond the lawn was that row of tall poinciana trees which her grandfather had planted, the enormous flower-sprays like delicate crimson lace against the dark green foliage . . .

'Well?' he demanded.

'Well — yes,' she said uncertainly.

'Look at it all.' He gave her another

shake. 'The trouble is, you can't see it, can you? Either you're so used to it, growing up out here, or you've been brainwashed — someone's been getting at you, not to see it — not to want to see it.' He drew in an angry breath and eyed her narrowly. 'And I bet I can put a name to that someone.'

'Don't!' she exclaimed vehemently.

'All right, I won't. But, Maggie, that marvellous colour, all that vibrant, singing life — it should shout glory hallelujah to you. But all your rigid little mind and eye can see is that stuff.' He gestured contemptuously in the direction of the paintings. 'These aren't you. Artistically, you're a hypocrite, do you know that? Why can't you let the real Maggie out?'

'These *are* the real Maggie,' she retorted hotly. Wrenching away from him, she crossed swiftly to the table to snatch up the nearest painting. 'This is me — this is how I paint.'

He looked at her in silence for a moment. 'You haven't understood one word of what I've been saying, have you?' He shook his head sadly. 'Ah, well, have it your way. I'll go and get changed.'

When he had gone, she let herself down into the nearest chair and stared unseeingly across the table, one hand fidgeting with the painting in front of her. Azalea mollis. After all her own niggling doubts, she'd been really pleased with this one, proud of the way she'd reproduced the silky sugar-pink petals.

Now he'd spoilt it — spoilt everything. Why had he chosen St Hilaire, out of all the islands in the Caribbean? Why had he come to Moon Creek? Why couldn't he have left her in peace? And why, above everything else, was it that they couldn't be together for more than five minutes without mentally gouging huge chunks out of each other?

A large, petulant tear ran down her cheek and dropped on to the white margin of the painting. She stared down at that spreading circle of wetness then thought, Oh, Maggie, you vowed you'd never shed a tear for a man again.

Well, she wouldn't. Fiercely, she brushed away another tear that was poised to plunge off her cheek and rammed back her chair. He wasn't going to ruin her enjoyment of her work. What did he know about painting, for heaven's sake? He was a musician, and everyone knew about musicians, didn't they? Yes, the best way to treat his remarks was with utter contempt.

She hadn't intended doing any more work today, but now she felt all at once the stabbing fear that he just might have undermined her confidence so much that that block might come back again. The panic was already rising in her as she went through to the room which had become her studio, but somehow she smothered it and took out her book of studies.

It was hard at first. Instead of the peony lutea, she kept seeing Steve's face, hearing his measured, lethal words, but gradually, blessedly, everything beyond the room, the paint and paper, faded to nothing.

8

Maggie put her hire car away in the garage and walked back to the house, feeling the afternoon sun scorch her neck and shoulders under the thin cream linen dress. Overhead, a tiny silver plane was climbing steeply away from the airport. The London flight.

She smiled and went on into the kitchen, where she poured herself a glass of lime juice, dropped in a couple of ice-cubes and sat at the table. She raised her glass in a private salute: here's to you, Maggie — and to those twenty paintings which, cocooned in white tissue and card, were winging their way to London.

But somehow, things were different this time. Oh, the relief was there, as usual — the relief of finishing a project and knowing she'd done it to the best of her ability. But something was lacking. In the old days, whenever she finished an assignment David would take her out for a celebration meal — champagne and all the trimmings. She smiled wryly. Well, if that was all that was missing, she'd found the key to her father's wine cellar, so there was nothing to stop her broaching half a dozen bottles of his best bubbly if she wanted.

But no, there was something else . . . And then, through the wall, came the sound of the piano. Of course, that was it. All at once, she had the urge to leap to her feet and hare round next door to tell Steve. She wanted him to seize her in a bear-hug, lifting her off her feet, and telling her what a clever girl she was. But, of course, he wouldn't tell her anything of the sort — just read her another lecture on her artistic inadequacies, no doubt.

All the same, though, she deserved a treat. In spite of all the hassle, she'd met the deadline, so now a little pampering was in order. She finished her drink and went upstairs to the bathroom.

All the bottles and jars she had bought in the chemist were lined up on the window-sill, hardly used. She'd spend the rest of the day on a full-scale beauty session, starting with a long, leisurely bath. While the water was running, she undressed then poured in a generous slurp of bubble bath, pinned up her hair and slid into the pink, scented water. Bliss. The millions of tiny bubbles caressed her skin, and gradually everything was lost in the perfumed haze which enveloped her . . .

She was floating idly, her big toes jammed into the taps, when dimly through the haze she heard running footsteps and the door was flung open.

'Get out!' she shrieked, cowering down in the water.

'What were you singing?'

'What?' Had he finally flipped his lid? 'I wasn't singing.'

'Yes, you were. What was it?'

'I don't know. And if I was, it wasn't

loud. I wasn't disturbing you, was I?' Terror almost made her squeak. If she really had disturbed him, any second now he was likely to snatch her up and fling her out on to the lawn.

'No, of course you weren't,' he snapped impatiently. 'I was on my way to the beach when I heard you.'

And now that she looked at him through the eddying steam, she saw that apart from a towel slung casually round his shoulders he was wearing nothing except a pair of very brief black trunks. She swallowed, and hastily fixed her gaze on the shower-head.

'Look, Maggie.' He was obviously reining himself in with a superhuman effort. 'You *were* singing.' He knelt down, put his arms on the bath and rested his chin on them, so that their faces were just six inches apart. 'So be a good girl and tell me what it was, and I'll leave you to enjoy your bubbles in peace.'

'I-I honestly can't remember,' she muttered, then, as he scowled at her, she cringed down even further under the waves.

'Hmm, that's a pity.'

'W-what do you mean?' Her voice quivered with apprehension, and almost too late she tried to get things back on a level footing. 'Now look here.' Metaphorically, she drew herself up to her full height — rather difficult as she was horizontal, and had to stay that way. 'You just get out of here. This is my half of the house.'

He lifted a finger and lazily twitched at the plug chain.

'W-what are you doing?'

'I'm going to stay here and watch all those lovely bubbles drain away.'

'You wouldn't dare.'

'Sure you can't remember?'

They exchanged a long, measuring look.

'This is intimidation, you know that?' she wailed. 'Infringement of personal liberties. There's a law here to deal with people like you. Just you wait till I get out.'

'But you're not getting out, are you, sweetie?' He pulled gently on the plug and she heard a faint gurgle, then he let it fall into place again. 'Because you can't remember.'

'Just go away, will you?' She smacked the water despairingly with her small fist.

'Think, Maggie.' She could almost feel him willing her to remember. '*Think*.'

Oh, lord, it really mattered to him, didn't it? Desperately, her mind ranged, like a hunted animal. What had been in her thoughts in that pink haze? Her paintings . . . the gallery . . . London . . . her student days, when, caught up in the intoxication of living, her feet had never seemed to touch the pavement. Pavement! That was it — she had it.

'Come on. You've got it!'

She'd tried to keep her face blank, but he was there as soon as she was. How well he knew her, she thought resentfully. In a month, he'd learned every nuance of her personality better than David had in six years. The Gemini factor coming out again perhaps — sharing this most tricky of birth signs seemed to put them permanently on the same wavelength.

'I think it was 'Scarborough Fair',' she said reluctantly.

'Sing it,' he commanded imperiously.

'What, *now*?'

'Yes.'

'But the water's getting cold,' she said sulkily.

'Never mind that. Just sing.'

He wasn't going to let her out until she had, she knew that. Self-consciously, she cleared her throat and, fixing her eye on the tiles opposite, began,

'Are you going to Scarborough Fair?
Parsley, sage, rosemary and thyme.'

She gave him a sideways glance. 'Was that it? It's a folk song I used to — '

'Yes, that's it.'

Exuberantly, he leapt to his feet, then, with a shout of triumph, scooped her up into his arms. Too astonished even to cry out, Maggie caught a glimpse of herself in the misty mirror, a small, rosy shape clasped in his bear-like embrace, and then he was kissing her full on the lips. It was a joyous, light-hearted kiss at first, but then, as her eyes closed and she put one hand up to his neck, he jerked back suddenly, stared at her for a moment, as though registering for the first time just what he was doing, then abruptly dropped her back into the bath.

Their gaze still held for an instant, then he said brusquely, 'Do you know any more folk songs?'

'Y-yes.' Something seemed to have got hold of her by the throat, so that she was having difficulty speaking. 'When I was a student, I — '

'Great. I want you next door in five minutes.' He looked round the room, picked up a bath towel and held it out to her. 'Put that on. Five minutes.'

She sat perfectly still, listening to his rapidly retreating footsteps. Her heart was pounding against her ribs and she felt dizzy, but she knew that it was not only the result of his sudden appearance or of her being snatched up out of a soothing bath. Rather, it was the realisation that, despite all her stern warnings to herself, yet again, before he had so abruptly shaken her free, she had been weakly surrendering to the intense pleasure of being held in his arms.

This thought was too disturbing to contemplate. In any case, five minutes, he'd said, and in his present mood if she didn't do as she was told he was quite capable of coming back for her and hauling her next door, just as she was. She leapt out of the bath and began frantically towelling herself.

* * *

'Where the devil have you been?'

Maggie, who had been congratulating herself that it had taken only six and a half minutes to dry herself, dress and comb her hair into a tight chignon, bit back her retort. He had put on that short black silk dressing-gown, but she was sure that under it he was still wearing nothing but his swimming briefs, so she was doubly grateful that she had taken the time to put on her most workmanlike shirt-dress in dark green cotton.

She allowed herself to be dragged across to the piano, where he sat down on the stool, folded his arms across his chest and looked at her.

'Now, sing.'

'But — I can't,' she protested.

He scowled. 'Why not?'

'Well, I — ' she floundered ' — I suppose I'd feel such a fool, singing in front of you. Look, I'll write down the words.'

'That's no good. You know it's the music I need.' He eyed her morosely. 'How come you know these folk songs, anyway? You weren't brought up in England.'

'No. I learned them while I was at

college.' She paused. 'If you must know, when we were students David taught them to me. He said they suited my voice — '

'I hate to agree with that swine in anything, but he's right.'

'And then we used to go busking — in the West End and round the pubs. He accompanied me on the violin, and a friend of his played the flute. We did very well — that's how I paid for my first trip home.'

'Well, then, if you can sing for a bar full of half-drunk strangers, I don't see why you can't sing for me.'

Don't you? she thought mutinously, but then she glanced down at him again. He was sitting, abstractedly swinging to and fro on the swivel stool, frowning down at the keyboard, and she realised suddenly how strained he looked, the crease between his brows more marked, the betraying tautness at the corners of his mouth. Caught up in their constant bickering and squabbling, she had all but forgotten the tremendous tension he was under. Her heart smote her, and impulsively she put her hand on one of his.

'All right, Steve, I'll try. Only, please, just tell me why you're so interested in English folk songs. Surely they're not your style.'

He looked up at her, a smile hovering at his lips. 'Because, my small, unpredictable ball of fire, it suddenly hit me when I heard you singing that that was the kind of music I'd been subconsciously searching for. I've tried my own compositions, soldiers' songs, World War One marches — you name it, I've tried it, but nothing worked.'

He reached for her, gently pulled her down on to his lap and sat, holding her to him, absently rubbing his chin against the top of her soft head. She felt her whole body tense as her heart beat in an alarming quickstep, but he seemed wholly taken up with his own thoughts.

'I've got it now, though. The hero's a

country boy, so if I can weave the songs
into a melody, accompanying him at his
work on the land, and then use them
again in the trenches, with his comrades
falling around him, the horror of the
guns, the mud, counterpointing the
earlier scenes at the plough and so on,
then it should make the point the
director's after.'

'I see,' she said slowly. Then, 'Well,
let's get started, shall we?'

' . . . Oh, don't deceive me. Oh,
   never leave me.
How could you use a poor maiden
   so?'

The song faded to silence. In the
little circle of lamplight, Steve leaned
forward to turn off the tape recorder,
ran the tape back and Maggie heard her
own voice, filling the room, husky and
vibrant. He listened for a moment,
nodded in satisfaction, then switched
off again.

Her head throbbing, she leaned

against the piano, flexing her aching legs. Outside it was quite dark, and when for the first time she glanced surreptitiously at her watch, her eyes widened with incredulity. 'Good grief, it's after eleven.' Her voice was hoarse from endless hours of singing.

'Is it?' But he was not really listening.

From the relative darkness of her part of the room, she stared across to where he was scribbling notes in his manuscript book with an old pencil stub.

'We haven't had anything to eat or drink.'

He glanced up briefly, seeming to focus on her with difficulty. 'What? Oh, yes — well, help yourself. There's plenty in the fridge.'

'Oh, no, I'm past eating. How about you?'

'Nothing for me.' She sensed the prickle of irritation behind the words.

'Well — I'll go then.'

'Yes — yes.' She was being dismissed with an impatient gesture of the hand.

Then, 'Oh, just one thing. Fetch me my cigarettes.'

'Certainly not. My chocolate for your cigarettes — that was what we agreed. And, in case you've got any plans, I've hidden them.'

He threw down his pencil. 'But you don't understand. I *must* have them. I can*not* work without them.'

'Sorry. They aren't good for you.'

'Oh, lord, preserve me from sanctimonious women. Just get them.'

He snatched up a book — a weighty *History of Modern Music* — and hurled it at her, but she just managed to dodge and skipped out of the room.

Ten minutes later, when she came back, he did not look up, merely grunted, 'Ah, good. Just put them there.'

Obediently, she set down on the table beside him the dish she was carrying. He regarded the contents with extreme disfavour.

'What the devil's this?'

'Raw carrots,' she said sweetly. 'I've

scraped them for you. When you feel that you need a smoke, chew one of these instead.'

She met his stony gaze unflinchingly and at last he growled, 'You're a hard taskmaster.'

'Me?' She rolled her eyes eloquently, her voice a little frog's croak, and he had the grace to grin guiltily.

'OK, sweetie — sorry.' He caught hold of her hand and gently brushed a kiss across her palm. 'Now, go away, there's a good girl.'

'But it's nearly midnight,' she protested. 'You ought to go to bed as well. You look exhausted.'

'Mmm.'

But he wasn't listening. He was barely aware that she was in the room. He was already shutting her out again, retreating into his private territory, the world not of Steve Donellan but of Stefan Barshinsky — a world where no one could follow.

Even as he retreated, though, she felt suddenly a terrible, wrenching longing to seize him in her arms, keep him with her. But instead, she lifted one hand, the hand which was still warm from the touch of his lips, and very softly laid it on his bent head then tiptoed soundlessly from the room.

Several times during the night she roused to hear the sound of the piano, and, once, her own voice, ghostly and disembodied. She finally woke just as it was getting light, opened the shutters and leaned out, drinking in long gulps of cool, flower-scented air, then she went still suddenly, staring down at the veranda.

Halfway along it a shaft of yellow light fell across the tiles, and when she peered down, she could see that the glass-panelled door stood ajar. He must still be working. Well, there were plenty of times when she'd worked right through the night when inspiration had finally struck. But even so, she was sure that he wouldn't have broken off, not even to get himself anything to drink.

Slipping on her cotton housecoat, she

went downstairs barefoot, unlocked her kitchen door and went out on to the terrace. Tentatively, she pushed open the door.

'Steve?'

But he was not there; only, the lamp was still on, and the piano legs were awash, ankle-deep, with screwed up papers. She surveyed the chaos with a faint smile, then turned to go. But now that she was here, she might as well tidy up for him. She went across the room for the waste-paper bin, then stopped dead.

He was here after all, stretched out full length on the delicate Sheraton *chaise-longue*, his head and one arm lolling over the edge.

'Steve?'

She leaned over him, speaking very softly, but he did not reply. His gentle, even breathing was warm against her cheek, and a feeling of immeasurable tenderness welled up inside her.

Looking round, she took up a rug from the floor, and covered him with it.

His head still lay awkwardly, though. She was about to fetch a pillow but instead she took off her housecoat, rolled it into a neat sausage, then stealthily lifted his head a fraction and slid it into place. He roused slightly, mumbling something unintelligible, but then relaxed back into sleep.

She knelt, looking down at him, then with one finger she gently traced the outline of his features. His brow; his cheeks, feeling the hard bones just beneath the surface; then finally, as her heart performed somersaults of terror, those sensitive lips.

He mumbled again, turned over violently, almost trapping her hand, and she leapt to her feet, switched off the lamp, and fled.

★ ★ ★

Over the next few days, she saw nothing of Steve. She found her housecoat on the patio one day when she came back from the beach, but otherwise he had

188

cut himself off completely, pulling his privacy round him like the shell of a hermit crab. Well, after all, she told herself, she'd come to Moon Creek for solitude, and that was precisely what she was having.

She spent a lot of her time down on the beach. He never appeared, and it was only her solitary trail of footprints which went to and from the water's edge. Several days, she even stayed on into the afternoon, although she always remained firmly inside her bikini, but he never came.

The piano was playing endlessly, and one morning she convinced herself that he wasn't eating. She made up a tempting plate of cold sliced chicken and salad, whipped some rum-soaked raisins and coffee into heavy cream, and sneaked in to put them at the front of his fridge where he couldn't fail to see them, but when she crept back that evening they were untouched.

The solitary days on the beach soon seemed to pall and she made several trips into Port Charlotte, visiting old schoolfriends. It was great to see them again and to catch up with all the island gossip. One afternoon, though, she came back from town feeling low and dispirited; she slumped down on the patio, her chin on her hands, staring listlessly across the garden.

What on earth was wrong with her — this vague 'not exactly ill, not exactly well' feeling that had been dogging her these last few days? There always was a reaction when she'd finished a difficult assignment, and of course she was waiting anxiously for a response from the gallery — but no, that wasn't it.

Ah, well, she might as well go in and change. She half rose from her chair, then stopped dead. Moon Creek — for the first time in her life, the house seemed empty and unwelcoming, and she thought suddenly, with painful clarity, I'm *lonely*, that's what it is. Maybe, after all, she was still missing David — perhaps the break with him had affected her even more than she'd realised.

Slowly, she went indoors and on upstairs. Halfway along the landing she paused, almost certain that she could hear faint sounds coming from the attics above. Perhaps it was a bird. In spite of her father blocking up all the holes under the eaves, they still sometimes managed to find their way in.

She climbed the narrow flight of stairs at the end of the corridor and opened the door. Sure enough, two of the small island sparrows had managed to get themselves trapped and were flying round in desperate circles, crashing against the walls. There was a skylight in the roof and she dragged an old leather trunk across, stood on it and after a struggle pushed the window open. The panic-stricken birds at last flung themselves at the oblong of blue, and she stood on tiptoe, watching them flutter away, before slowly closing the skylight and getting down, wiping the dust from her hands.

As she bent to push the trunk back, she saw that on the top were gold-tooled letters: M.V.F. Marguerite Victoria Forsythe — her great-grandmother. Maggie stared down at them. This was probably her school trunk; she'd had a governess, Maggie knew, until she was sixteen, when she'd been sent to a finishing school in Switzerland which had, at the time, an excellent reputation for turning wild, undisciplined tomboys into genteel, well-behaved young ladies.

They'd been successful in Marguerite Victoria's case apparently, and yet, looking at the old sepia wedding photograph — and even the full-length portrait that hung in the sitting-room downstairs — Maggie had always privately suspected that behind that sveltely elegant face there lay a hint of mischief, while more than a touch of the devil lurked in those grey eyes, shadowed by a crown of red-gold hair.

Maggie slipped to her knees, and

turning the key in the rusty lock, inched open the hinges. She had expected the trunk to be filled with old books and papers, but instead there were tissue-wrapped bundles, and a faint, spicy smell of cinnamon and cloves drifted up from them.

Wonderingly, she opened the first package and then gasped as, between her fingers, she felt the cool drift of silk. It was a white, full-length petticoat, every tiny stitch hand-sewn, the bust cups covered with the most exquisitely worked lace she had ever seen. It was weightless, like a white cloud of perfection.

Hardly breathing, she put it aside, reached for the next bundle and drew out a tiny camisole top, this time in palest cream silk, with a pair of matching, knee-length drawers, embroidered with little cupid's hearts and bows.

More lingerie followed, all fragile works of art with no more substance than a spider's web, and, finally, two white nightdresses, one of silk, the other in finest broderie anglaise, each with its matching négligé.

There was a discreet label inside each of them, the name of a Paris *couturier*, and at last Maggie understood. All the female members of her family in the nineteenth century had had their wedding trousseaus sent from Paris; this was Marguerite Victoria's. A tight ache in her throat, she held up the silk négligé, looking at it through a sudden blur of tears, then very carefully wrapped it again.

Lying in the lid of the trunk were the camisole and drawers. She reached down for them but then, on a sudden impulse, stood up, tugged off the loose sundress she was wearing and pulled on the silk top. It slid down over her warm, bare skin like cool water, and when she looked down at herself she saw how the narrow straps and low-cut, straight bodice set off the line of her shoulders, half revealing, half suggesting the full curve of her breasts, while the cream colour gave a pearly glow to her skin. Just for a moment, she hesitated, then slipped into the drawers.

In the corner was an old cheval swivel mirror, and she pirouetted over to stand in front of it, gazing at this totally new Maggie. Catching up her rumpled hair with one hand, she put on a deliberately provocative pout, arching her body and laughing irrepressibly at herself.

But then the laugh died. She heard footsteps as someone rapidly mounted the narrow stairs, then a voice called, 'Maggie, are you up there?' and Steve burst into the room.

9

Steve halted abruptly when he saw Maggie and she too seemed to freeze, one hand to her throat, her hair tumbling back unnoticed to her shoulders. The shaft of light from the upper window fell behind him, and she saw the tiny motes of dust which he had disturbed dancing in the air above him and settling on his blue cotton shirt and pale straw-coloured hair.

'I thought I heard you up here.'

It was a flat statement, but there was a *frisson* of something in his voice which simultaneously terrified and thrilled her.

'I — I came up to let out some birds that were trapped, and I found this trunk. These clothes — they're from Paris.' She knew she was babbling, but could not stop. 'I think they're my great-grandmother's — you know, the one in the photo, with the — '

' — frangipani. Yes, I remember.'

Those dark, inscrutable eyes regarded her flushed face, took in her body, hardly more than half-masked by the fragile silk, then went back to her face. The tension was stirring again, rousing out of the dark corners where it had lain in wait for them both. He made no effort to touch her — in fact, he had jammed his hands hard into the pockets of his denim shorts — and yet she could feel the force of his desire reach out to her, demanding that she surrender to him.

Her blood was congealing thickly in her veins, her pulse beat rapid and erratic. As she watched, mesmerised, he slowly moved towards her. He stopped just in front of her and for long moments they stared into each other's eyes, seeing their tiny golden reflections in the dilated pupils, then with a muffled groan he caught hold of her, dragging her into his arms.

She felt his lips fasten hungrily on

hers, then at last release them to trail across her cheek and down her throat, to where the pulse fluttered under her skin. Closing her eyes, she arched her neck against his hot, searching mouth, and put her arms round him, her nails digging roughly into his shoulders.

One hand, clasped in the small of her back, held her hard against him, while the other moved beneath the flimsy top to fasten on one breast. Lowering his head, he nuzzled the silk away, then his tongue was circling the breast to settle finally on the taut centre. His other hand was sending tingling shivers up her spine as it moved lower and lower until he eased his way beneath the waistband of the drawers. His fingers splayed across the soft flesh of her buttocks, clasping her to him until she could feel the power of his desire.

'Steve — Steve.' It was a sigh, which thundered inside her.

But then, a voice, even deeper within her, was crying out that this was madness, utter madness. Her whole body tensed, and at that very same moment his hands loosed their grasp and he was thrusting her away from him, so violently that she would have fallen if he had not caught hold of her again, his grip so painful that it brought stinging tears to her eyes.

'Oh, Maggie.' His voice, his entire body, was trembling with the struggle to subdue himself and he could barely speak. 'I swore I would never lay a finger on you again. But then, when I saw you — ' He shook her. 'Oh, lord, why did you have to wear those things? I'm sorry.'

'It — it doesn't matter,' she whispered. Desolation was washing over her, and he had to bend towards her to hear the words. 'I — just wish you hadn't come up here.'

Tremors were rising through her too, shaking her whole body, and he must have felt them for, with an inarticulate groan, he pulled her to him, whispering, 'No, it's all right,' as she flinched away. He held her against him, one arm round her, the other cradling her head to his chest, until gradually the dreadful shaking faded.

Gently, he pushed her away a little and looked down at her, his dark eyes sombre. 'I didn't intend for this to happen, Maggie, believe me.' He gave her a wry smile. 'But I guess it's no use pretending to each other any longer.'

'Pretending?' she murmured.

He put up his hand and with one finger softly traced the outline of her full mouth. 'That we're not sexually attracted to one another. For me, I want you more desperately than I've ever wanted any woman — my ex-wife included. Yes,' as she looked up at him, wide-eyed, 'but a relationship with you — well, it just wouldn't work out, for either of us. What you need is total commitment — marriage. Anything less would be wrong for you, but me,' his mouth tightened, 'I'm wholly incapable — well, all right, unwilling — to give any woman that again.'

Maggie nodded sadly. 'Yes, you're

right. I suppose we're both prisoners of our pasts. You've had your fill of marriage, and I — I don't want any more affairs.'

'Anyway,' he loosed her gently, 'life's been complicated enough these last few weeks. I reckon it would be quite impossible to have two full-blown artistic egoists living permanently under the same roof — and both Geminis, at that.'

She knew he was trying to lift her from her mood. 'Yes, Steve, you're quite right. We must both keep away from each other — in that way, at least — from now on. After all, Moon Creek ought to be big enough for both of us.' Somehow, she managed a pale smile. 'But anyway, talking of being under the same roof, why did you come up here?'

'Oh, I came to see if you'd like to listen to what I've managed so far. It's funny, you know,' he gave her one of his rare, beautiful smiles, 'normally, I won't let anyone near me till a work is completely finished — superstitious dread, I suppose — but somehow, that doesn't apply to you.'

'Oh, I'd love to, Steve — thank you.' She was almost overwhelmed by his invitation.

'Well, it's only fair, after all.' He was still defusing the emotions that clung to them. 'You let me tear your paintings apart, so the least I can do is let you loose on my music.' His gaze took in the scattered garments lying beside the trunk, but he did not look at her again. 'Come round when you're ready.'

'Let me just pack these things away.'

She knelt down beside the trunk again. It was almost empty; only one small bundle remained. She lifted it out and pulled back the tissue, then sniffed at where the faint scent seemed still to cling to the brown, withered petals.

'What is it?'

She jumped. She thought he'd gone, but when she glanced round he was looking down at her.

'It's frangipani,' she said tightly. 'It must be some of the flowers from her wedding garland.'

He came down on his haunches beside her and took the flowers from her. 'Marguerite's wreath,' he said softly, and, wrapping them in their tissue again, carefully replaced them.

★   ★   ★

'Thanks.'

Maggie smiled at the counter clerk then walked out of the Post Office, the flimsy blue airmail letter clutched in her palm. Somehow, she resisted the impulse to tear it open in the middle of the car park, and even when she was back in the car she stared down at it, flicking it against the steering-wheel, before slitting open the seams with her ignition key . . .

She was driving past the front of the house when Steve appeared on the veranda. She hesitated for a moment; since that day in the attic, she'd scarcely seen him — it was as if they were avoiding one another even more. But she just had to tell somebody, and there was no one else.

Braking hard, in a spurt of gravel, she seized the letter and leapt out. He stood on the steps, watching her, and as she came up to him she was even more forcibly aware of the constraint which had grown between them. Somehow, though, she managed a bright smile.

'Hi, Steve. How are you?'

'Oh, fine.' But he still looked tired, and the heavy stubble on his unshaven chin gave him an endearingly vulnerable expression. And yet surely the film score was making headway now — he'd certainly seemed pleased with the first drafts he'd played for her the other afternoon.

'How's the music coming on?' she asked.

He shrugged. 'OK. How's the painting?'

'Oh, all right,' she began, but then, unable to contain her excitement a moment longer, she brandished the letter, her eyes shining. 'It's from

Marcus — he owns the gallery in London. He loves the paintings — ' she could not resist a sneaky sideways look at him ' — and he wants me to do a dozen more, for a range of up-market greetings cards he's bringing out.'

Steve gave a whoop. 'Oh, that's terrific, Maggie. Congratulations!' For a moment she thought he was going to sweep her up jubilantly in his arms, but then he went on, 'This calls for a drink. Come on inside.'

She followed him into the sitting-room where he poured out two rum and gingers.

'Well, here's to you, Maggie,' he raised his glass to her, 'and to the next assignment.' As she lifted her glass in return, he went on, 'Does this mean you'll be going back to England?'

'Oh, I hadn't really thought about it,' she said slowly. 'I suppose so.' But even as she spoke, the realisation hit her that she did not want to leave Moon Creek — she couldn't bear to. 'I may not have to, though. I didn't use all my working studies in the last batch of pictures.'

'So it'll be more of the same, then.'

She looked at him, her eyes narrowing slightly, then hating herself for the defensive note she heard in her voice, said, 'Of course. As you see, some people appreciate my paintings. Marcus is sure they'll sell very well.'

'And are you going to spend your whole life producing something just because it happens to sell well?'

'If I want to, yes,' she replied belligerently.

'But a painting — any work of art — should reflect the personality of the artist.'

'And you know my personality, do you?'

'Yes, I think so,' he said levelly.

Maggie stared at him, chewing her lip. She had to put a stop to this — *now*, before he ruined everything again. She stood up. 'Thank you for the drink. I'll go and put the car away.'

'No. Hang on a minute. Let me try and show you what I mean.'

Totally mystified, she sat down again, listening as he ran upstairs two at a time, then, a few moments later, he came hurtling back down. He was carrying two large oil paintings.

'These were hanging in my room upstairs.' He put them down on to the table. 'Come over here.'

Reluctantly, Maggie went across and, with a curious feeling twisting at her insides, stared down at the pictures.

'Now, this flower study, first. They're — what are they called?'

'Canna lilies,' she said quietly.

'That's it. Well, just look at those colours — the crimson, the orange, the flame. Those flowers — they're like Van Gogh's 'Sunflowers'. They look as if they're about to leap off the canvas at you. There's more life in one petal of these than in the whole of — ' He broke off abruptly. 'And look at this one.'

He held it up to her, and she saw a group of figures on a beach, fishermen pulling in their nets.

'See how they're silhouetted against

the white sand — and the movement — look at that figure there. You can almost feel their muscles rippling.' He swung round to her. 'Maggie, can't you see it — the life, the vibrancy? Why can't *you* paint like this?'

'Well, actually, I can — *I* painted them.'

'What?'

She'd set out to stop him in his tracks, and boy, had she succeeded. 'Or, at least,' she went on, 'I could once. I did these — oh, ten years ago, before I went to London.'

He was still looking at her, quite astounded. That had knocked some of the wind out of his sails, she thought with satisfaction. Perhaps now he'd leave her alone.

He spoke at last. 'I should have guessed.' He eyed her thoughtfully. 'Spunky, sparky, maddening — but full of life. Well, that settles it.'

Settles what? She didn't altogether care for the way he was looking at her. 'W-what do you mean?' Nervously, she edged away from him as, too late, she realised that her rash admission just might have brought a hornets' nest down on her head.

'This.'

There was a brief, wholly unequal wrestling match, then she found herself tucked ignominiously under one arm. Hurling punches and abuse, she was carried through the hall and up the stairs. There was no time for coherent thought, but just once it did cross her mind that she seemed to have spent an awful lot of time lately being dragged around Moon Creek by this, this —

'Right. In here.'

He pushed open a door and dumped her on her feet in the middle of one of the rooms at the unused end of the house. She glowered at him through her tangle of hair.

'What the hell do you think you're doing?'

He regarded her grimly. 'I was right about you, Maggie Sanderson — you are a little hypocrite. Inside you, you've got all that vitality, but you refuse to let it come out. Well, I'm going to help you.'

'And just how do you intend doing that?' The would-be defiance in her voice could not mask her anxiety.

'You're going to try painting the way you used to.'

'But I can't.' Her stomach was churning with alarm. 'I told you, that was ten years ago, when I was still a teenager. My style's matured since then, and I can't go back.'

'You can at least try.'

'No, I won't,' she hurled at him. 'Who do you think you are — Svengali? If you think I'm going to allow myself to be influenced by you . . . '

Her voice tailed away at the terrifying thought of what that might mean — perhaps releasing all kinds of emotions that she had to keep stamped down out of sight. Feverishly, she sought escape. 'Besides, I've only got my water-colour gear with me. I can't possibly — '

'Is that so?' he drawled, and before she could move he was out of the room, the key had turned in the lock and she heard him going off down the corridor.

When he returned five minutes later he was carrying an easel, a bundle of blank canvases and a battered straw beach bag filled with oil paints, turps and brushes.

'I came across these some time ago in that cupboard under the stairs. They wouldn't be yours, by any chance?'

'They might be,' she muttered.

'Good. That solves that little problem, then.'

A paint-stained overall was slung from his shoulder and, taking hold of it, he advanced on her. 'Now, be a good girl.'

Maggie scowled at him, but there was no point in struggling, so she allowed herself to be helped into it.

'Come over to the window.' She followed him across and gazed out stonily. 'Now, look out there — look at the hills, the trees, rolling down to the sea.'

She shook her head stubbornly. 'I shan't paint them. I don't do landscapes any more.'

'Well, if you must paint flowers — ' he opened the window, leaned out and broke off a flowering spray from the poinciana tree growing alongside the house ' — try this.'

'I — ' Maggie began, then stopped. A slow smile crossed her face, and she hastily bent over the scarlet flowers. 'Oh, all right, Steve,' she murmured submissively, 'you win.'

She was pleased with the note of docility she had managed to infuse into her voice, but she dared not look up to meet those penetrating eyes.

'Good girl,' he said. 'I'm afraid I'll still have to lock you in — just in case you change your mind — but I'll be back at lunchtime.'

Ten minutes later, Maggie eased herself down from the lowest branch of the poinciana and began to make her way cautiously towards the corner of the house. The poor sap, he'd be back at work by now; her car keys were still in the ignition, so she'd be off and away before he suspected a thing. How he'd react when he found out — well, she'd just have to face that when —

As she rounded the corner, she cannoned into something hard and unyielding.

'You!' Steve roared. 'You crafty little devil — I might have known!'

And snatching her up again, with even less ceremony, he strode into the house. This time, he carried her upstairs to a smaller room, at the other end of the landing. It was the old nursery, and she did not need to look to know that there were iron bars at the window.

'Don't you dare move,' he ordered, and within a minute he was back with all her equipment.

'I suppose you intend to starve me into submission,' she snarled.

He gave a mirthless laugh. 'That's a

very good idea. A few days on bread and water might just knock some sense into you.'

'Oh, you — you overgrown ape, you!' she yelled, and snatching up a handful of wooden bricks from the toy box beside her, hurled them after his retreating back.

When he had gone, she paced stormy-eyed around the room, then slumped against the wall in one corner beside the beautiful old rocking-horse she had ridden as a child. She put her arms round his wooden neck and laid her face against the scratchy mane.

'Oh, Dobbin,' she whispered miserably, 'why does life have to be so complicated now?'

At last, she straightened up and wandered over to the window. She opened it and stood leaning her hot forehead against the bars, letting her eyes drift aimlessly across the scene outside. Inland, the blue cone-shaped hills shimmered under the late morning sun, their lower slopes masked by dense tropical forest.

It would be quite tricky to capture the nuances of colour — the blues of the hills, the sky and the sea, for instance — they were all subtly different. She found her hand straying to the bag which contained her paints, and caught herself up, horrified. But then she thought, Oh, what the heck? If she didn't produce something, he was quite capable of keeping her a prisoner here, like Bluebeard. She was stubborn enough, but if it came to any battle of wills, she knew who'd come off second-best.

Sitting down at the table, she pulled out her old palette and began hunting through her paint tubes. Flake white . . . sienna brown . . . vermilion . . . They were like old friends she hadn't seen for years.

She got up, pulled the easel across to the window, and placed a canvas on it, then stood, alternately gazing critically out at the distant hills and frowning down at the canvas. As well as the blues, she'd need lots of dark, intense greens, with here and there a flash of colour. And then a focal point — that scarlet tree-hibiscus, perhaps . . .

★ ★ ★

Maggie set down her brush and straightened her aching shoulders. Her right hand, which had been gripping her brushes, prickled with pins and needles and as she flexed her fingers she winced as the blood flowed painfully back.

She felt totally drained, her mind beyond any sensation except exhaustion, but gradually she began to realise first that she was very thirsty, and then that it was almost too dark to see her painting. When had he put her in here? She pressed her hand to her throbbing forehead. About eleven, wasn't it? And now — she peered at her watch in disbelief — it was after six!

She looked out of the window. The

hills had vanished; only the last glow of sunset was turning the sea to pale apricot. She walked stiffly across to the door and flicked the light switch, but nothing happened — the bulb must have gone.

Heavens, she was thirsty. Her lips were parched, her mouth was dry as ashes. Why hadn't he come? He'd said he'd be back at lunchtime, hadn't he? She knocked on the door, rather self-consciously at first, but then, when there was no response, she hammered on it with the flat of her hand. When she stopped to listen, though, there were no answering footsteps.

She tried to call 'Steve,' but her voice came out as little more than a croak. Where was he? Angry now, she took off her sandal and pounded on the floor, but still there was no reply, so in the end she sat on the window-sill, willing herself to patience.

As the first stars appeared, though, the temperature began to fall rapidly and she huddled down on the mattress of the little cot bed in the corner. Mosquitoes were buzzing around her, homing in on her bare arms and legs, and she slapped ineffectually at them . . .

She woke from a confused half-waking dream, where she had been drawing water from a well only to have it turn to fine dust, to see the pale moonlight on her face. When she looked at her watch she saw, with dull misery, that it was almost midnight. He just didn't care whether she lived or died.

Listlessly, she heard a door bang somewhere downstairs, then there were running feet and, as she still lay, only half aware, the door was flung open.

'Maggie!' His voice was harsh with alarm, and she heard the light switch click uselessly. 'For heaven's sake, where are you?'

'Over here,' she whispered through chalk-dry lips, and he swiftly crossed the room to kneel beside her.

'Oh, honey, are you all right? I forgot all about you.'

He'd forgotten her. How could he have done? She lay looking up at him, then her lips quivered and, pressing the back of her hand to her mouth, she began to cry softly. Steve gathered her to him, his face ravaged.

'Oh, hell — don't. I'm so sorry, baby. I've been working, right up to now.'

'But I knocked. Didn't you hear me?'

He gave her a tight smile. 'Fighting with you about your painting — I don't know what it's done for you, but it seemed to release something in me. I've spent all day wandering in the grounds, composing in my mind, then tonight I've been trying to get it all down on paper.'

'S-so the film score's really taking shape?'

'No, not that.' Then, as she sensed his reluctance, 'It's something I've had in my mind for some time now.'

Her snuffles had subsided and he very gently lifted her to her feet, then surveyed her in the pale light. 'Come on. I'll carry you.'

'No — no, I'm all right now.'

She managed a faint, rueful smile as she croaked the words, but he swung her up into his arms and she lay back, not quite tired enough to be unaware of the sensation of her body against his, her cheek nestled to his chest, the comforting strength of his arms around her.

He set her down on the sofa in the sitting-room then fetched a jug of lime water, poured her a brimming glass and sat watching her closely as she drained it. She wiped her mouth with the back of her hand.

'Wonderful.'

'More?'

'Yes, please.'

'Something to eat?'

'Oh, no, thank you.' She was past hunger. As he refilled her glass, she remembered something. 'Oh — my painting.'

'You mean you've done one?'

'Yes. I don't think it's very good, but — '

'Shall I fetch it?' He hesitated. 'Are you sure you want me to see it?'

She smiled up at him. 'Yes, I'd like you to.'

He came back with it and stood under the lamp, studying it intently. He said nothing though, and at last she asked tentatively, 'What do you think of it? My oils technique is really rusty, so — '

'It's marvellous, absolutely marvellous,' he said slowly, then flashed her a little grin. 'There you are. You *can* still do it — I knew you could.'

'Yes, Svengali,' she said meekly, though with a sideways look.

He pulled a face. 'No, Maggie. You did it, and nobody else. I might have been a cruel, unfeeling swine and locked you up, but I haven't imposed something on you that wasn't there. All I've done is help you uncover what's been there, deep down, all along.'

She got up and stood beside him, looking critically at the painting. 'Hmm, perhaps you're right.' But the need to retain her independence, not to submit entirely to his will, reasserted itself, and she added determinedly, 'But even if I do any more, I'm not going to give up my water-colours entirely.'

'Nobody's asking you to.' He smiled wryly. 'I'm sure your friend Marcus certainly wouldn't thank me if you did — but if you paint any more oils, maybe he'd like to see them too.'

'Yes, he might do,' she said slowly. 'Perhaps if I did a series — '

'But not tonight,' he said firmly. 'Do you want another drink?'

She shook her head.

'Well, in that case,' he rumpled her red-gold hair, but then dropped his hand abruptly, 'come on, it's time you were tucked up in bed.'

10

'Steve, I was wondering . . . '

He glanced up briefly from the table. 'Yes?'

His tone was definitely not welcoming, but Maggie forced herself to advance into the room. He frowned up at her, and she thought with a sudden pang that they had become strangers again — no, worse than strangers. He had been working at his score — often in the evenings, as she prowled restlessly around the grounds, she had heard her simple folk songs, transformed now into melodies which tugged at her heart with their bittersweet poignancy — while every day she had been painting.

She had made several attempts at the water-colour studies, but each time had pushed them aside and turned back to her oils. She had worked indoors, in her studio, but more and more she was taking her canvases outside, into the grounds and down on to the beach, striving to capture the vibrant tropical life all round her.

She'd found herself painting with ever-increasing intensity, as if to make up for lost time, piling the paint on the canvas, sometimes in her impatience throwing aside her brushes and layering it on with her palette knife or even her fingers. It was as though the missing link between her eye and the image — her heart maybe? — had fused, and the joy of creativity, which had been absent for so long, was now unfolding within her like a flower.

But until today she'd carefully avoided any contact with Steve, and she was rapidly beginning to wish that she'd left it that way.

'I — er, I wondered if you'd like to come round for a meal tomorrow evening?'

He finally seemed to accept that she was not going to retreat, and laid down his pencil. 'Tomorrow evening?'

'Yes — you know. *Tomorrow*,' she said meaningfully, then laughed. 'You've forgotten, haven't you? It's your birthday.'

'Good grief, so it is.' He clapped his hand to his forehead. 'But how the devil did you know?'

'Oh,' she flushed guiltily, 'if you must know, I looked you up in a music reference book in Charlotte library.' But she couldn't possibly tell him how strange it had seemed to pore over all the bald details of his life, even down to his marriage. Not his divorce, though — the book had been compiled several years previously. Instead, she went on, 'With your being a Gemini, I knew it must be soon.'

'Thirty-six.' He grimaced. 'Maybe I'd do better to forget all about it. Work all day and right through the night might be the best way to celebrate it.'

'No!' Maggie was quite shocked. 'You mustn't do that,' she added vehemently, then unaccountably felt tears sting her eyes at the dismal picture. What a soft fool she was becoming. If he wanted to ignore his birthday completely, well, that was his privilege.

'Thank you, Maggie.' He was watching her, his eyes grave. 'I'd be delighted to come.'

'Oh, good.' She gave him a dazzling smile, then turned away.

'And it must be yours soon?'

'Oh, yes, in a couple of weeks.' She hesitated, then went on uncertainly, 'Well, I mustn't disturb you any longer. How's it coming?'

'I've almost finished — this stage, anyway. Enough to get back up to LA to start working with the director, marrying my drafts to the film itself.'

'So you'll be leaving soon?'

'Mmm. Pretty soon.'

Their glances met, then skimmed away quickly.

'I'll leave you to it, then,' she said. 'Tomorrow evening, about seven.'

★ ★ ★

Maggie carefully poured the cheese soufflé mixture into the dish, sprinkled parmesan and cayenne over it, then slid it into the oven on the shelf above the fillet steak which, stuffed with mushrooms and wrapped in a puff pastry case, was just beginning to colour nicely. By the time they'd had a drink — one of her father's bottles of Dom Perignon was already on ice — the soufflé would be ready.

She fidgeted with the pink hibiscus heads, already in place on the china pedestal dish, and the half-dozen rather tatty birthday candles and holders she had found in a drawer. Then, for the sixth time, she checked in the fridge that the chocolate freezer cake was still perfect; she'd found the recipe when, on a sudden inspiration, she'd dug out her mother's battered copy of the *Fannie Farmer Boston Cookbook*.

Strange how she'd so enjoyed planning this meal. For years she'd hated cooking, but preparing a birthday dinner for Steve, who so obviously appreciated good food, was somehow different, more satisfying. Smiling to herself, she went upstairs to dress.

She had showered earlier and washed her hair, leaving it loose on her shoulders. Now she only had to put on a little pink lip-gloss, mascara, and some of the light grey shadow which brought out the brilliant depths of her eyes — not that she really needed it, she thought, studying her reflection. Tonight, there was a soft glow about her which made her beautiful. And yet — she wasn't beautiful, not usually. So . . . ?

She shied away from the question, and turned to the dress which lay across the bed. She had bought it only that morning, after discarding every other outfit in despair and haring off into town. Slipping it on, she stood before the mirror, turning slowly to see herself from all angles. It had been horribly expensive, but, she'd told herself stoutly, it was no more than she deserved for all her hard work.

The fine jade-green silk clung to her

body, moving as she moved, while the simple bodice, with its two narrow shoulder-straps, perfectly set off her slender throat, lightly tanned shoulders, and her hair, which shimmered like molten fire. She gazed at herself a moment longer, then went back downstairs, the excitement flickering inside her like the summer lightning she could see far out on the horizon, and sat on the patio to wait for Steve . . .

★ ★ ★

A moth blundered against the candle-lamp beside her, making her jump. She brushed it away to safety, then glanced once more at her watch. Gone nine. He wasn't coming.

She got up stiffly from the bamboo chair, the depression and anger warring inside her. She certainly wasn't going round to him again. At eight o'clock, half wondering if he was ill or something, she'd gone, only to find him bent over his manuscript book. When she'd hesitantly asked if he was coming soon, he'd stared at her as though he'd never set eyes on her in his life before.

'Yes, yes, OK,' he'd snapped at last, the irritability crackling like static electricity in his voice. 'Just give me a couple of minutes, will you?'

And that had been over an hour ago. She went through to the kitchen and opened the oven door. The beautiful soufflé still sat on its shelf, shrunken and leathery. Snatching it out, she threw it into the sink, scarcely registering the crack as the ovenproof glass came into contact with the cold metal. The pastry around the beef looked like dark mahogany; she took it outside and hurled it into the darkness. No doubt something would appreciate it, even if *he* didn't.

She stood, staring after it, the tight little fist of misery clenching in her stomach, then thought, No. No tears — he's not worth tears. Instead, she'd storm round there and tell him exactly what she thought of him. But then she stopped dead, gnawing on her lip. What was the use? He'd either curtly dismiss her with that cold, forbidding look of his again — or, even worse, insist on coming back with her, all empty apologies, now that it was too late.

As she turned back she caught sight of the large, gift-wrapped package, lying in one of the bamboo chairs. She stared at it, the desolation welling inside her, then went indoors to clear away. But the sight of the debris, alongside the flowers and the pathetic little candles, was too much. Snatching up her keys, she ran headlong across the yard to her car . . .

★   ★   ★

Maggie didn't know how long she was away. All she knew was that she had been driving, almost blindly, criss-crossing the island on the rocky inland tracks, until exhaustion had finally forced her to turn for home. By her hours of reckless driving, she had hoped to cauterise her feelings, but as she stood staring at Moon Creek, silhouetted in the brilliant moonlight, the slow fuse of anger still burned within her.

She had almost reached the veranda when she froze. Steve was sitting on the steps, his head leaning against the pillar. When he saw her, he got slowly to his feet. But she couldn't face him — not now. Any confrontation might so easily end with her breaking down in tears, she knew that, and that would be the final humiliation.

She swung away from him, but he caught hold of her wrist.

'Maggie.'

'No, Steve.' She was struggling frantically to break free.

'You must let me explain.'

Must she? Must she listen to more male excuses, designed to convince her that it was actually she who was in the wrong? She'd had enough of those from other people.

Wrenching her hand free, she measured the distance to the house, in the same split second realised she would never make it, and instead turned to run. She ran blindly across the grass, zig-zagging wildly, with no coherent thought of where she was going, only that she had to get away from him.

Finally, her breath sobbing in her ears, she plunged into the darkness of the overhanging trees and pulled up. There was no sound behind her. She'd thrown him off — or perhaps he hadn't even bothered to chase after her.

She turned slowly and, with a gasp of shock, bumped straight into him.

'What the hell did you run off like that for?' He seized her roughly, but then almost in the same instant, dropped his grasp, to run his hand through his hair. 'Look, Maggie, I'm sorry — '

'*Sorry!*' All the angry misery which had been smouldering for hours inside her burst into white-hot fury. 'Is that all you can say, you — you self-centred pig, you? You're incapable of considering anybody except your precious self.

No wonder your wife — '

'Shut up, damn you!'

He made a grab for her but she ducked back and, way past any rational thought now, brought her hand up to strike him. He caught hold of it, savagely wrenching it down, until a cry of pain was dragged from her. As she fought for breath — and self-control — he stared blankly down at her for an instant, then gave a long, shuddering sigh.

'Oh, Maggie.'

She put up her free hand, though whether to reach out to him or ward him off, she had no clear idea. He caught it, burying his lips in her small palm, his teeth bared against her hot skin, until her fingers curved around his face and her eyes closed as she felt the desire surge through her veins, igniting every part of her.

As she gasped with the jolting shock of it, he straightened and pressed his mouth to hers with fierce possessiveness. His fingers tangled in her long strands of hair, he trailed greedy, burning kisses all over her face and throat, until a violent shudder shook her. He must have felt it for he groaned something unintelligible, then she felt his hands searching out the zip of her dress.

He tore it open, then, holding her away from him a fraction, he ripped the dress down and with one fluid movement pulled her clear of it and her panties. She reached for him and, too impatient to undo his shirt, slid her hands up under it, the touch of his warm, smooth back setting alight little flames of sensuality at her fingertips. Amid all the tropical night scents she was becoming drunk on the potent male aroma of his body, so that her senses reeled and she dug her hands into his back.

Next moment, he swung her up into his arms, lifting her high so that he could kiss her rounded breasts until they swelled in ecstasy to meet his suckling mouth. Raising her even higher, he let his lips graze across her stomach, trailing that trail of fire lower, ever lower, until it fused with the molten heat at her very centre.

'Oh, Steve — please.'

It was a breathless little sigh, but though caught up in the intensity of his passion he heard her. Still holding her, he knelt down then laid her on the ground. He stood for a moment, peeling off his own clothes, then, as he came down to her again, she went into his arms in total surrender.

Already half consumed by the passions which raged through them both, they had no time for gentle, measured lovemaking. He came into her fiercely, and she felt her body open to him so that all her senses filled with him, as at last the stoked fires within her blazed free, exploding into fragments to throw the incandescent flames high into the sky above them . . .

★   ★   ★

Maggie stirred, and felt his arms curve round her. He said something against her ear.

'Mmm?' It was a sleepy murmur and he laughed softly, nipping the delicate lobe between his teeth.

'Nothing. Just — Maggie.' He buried his face in her hair. 'You're so alive, so vital — even your hair.' As he ran his fingers along a silky, newly washed strand, she heard the faint crackle of static. 'And you smell absolutely wonderful.'

'No, that isn't me.'

She propped herself on her elbow, inhaling the luscious perfume which had been teasing at her senses too. Then she gave a gasp of astonishment. 'Oh, Steve. It's the frangipani — we're lying under the trees.'

In her headlong dash to escape him, she must have blundered into their dense shade, quite unthinking of where she was, and after that — the scarlet flared in her cheeks as she remembered the wild, almost primitive nature of their lovemaking.

The night wind stirred, sending a shower of tiny pale flowerlets down on them, and she shivered — only slightly, but he felt it.

'Come on. You'll catch cold.'

He stood up, drawing her up with him, then, taking his shirt, wrapped her in it before slipping into his trousers. Then he picked up her discarded dress, which lay in a tangle at their feet, and, putting his arm round her, he steered her out from among the trees.

Once out on the grass, though, he dropped his arm to his side. They walked towards the house in silence, and something about that silence began to oppress Maggie's spirits. For better or worse, their relationship was changed, and now she desperately needed Steve to reassure her, but when she sneaked a sidelong glance at him he was frowning, as though engrossed in his own thoughts, and a dreadful heaviness settled on her.

At the patio he halted and, taking her

hand, softly brushed his lips across it. 'Maggie.'

But he was looking down at her palm, not her, and she knew with terrible clarity that he regretted bitterly what had happened.

'Don't — don't say anything, Steve,' she said unsteadily and pulled her hand away, willing him to go, now. But he followed her up the steps, and as she crossed the terrace she saw the package, still on the bamboo chair. She hesitated fractionally, then picked it up and thrust it at him. 'Happy birthday.'

'Oh — thank you.' He took it from her, but he was clearly disconcerted by her sudden gesture. 'Am I to open it now?'

'If you want.'

She forced herself to speak lightly, but he walked into the sitting-room and flicked on the light. As she leaned against the wall, watching him, he ran his finger under the sticky tape and pulled back the wrapping-paper.

He was silent for so long that, even

though she had vowed that she wouldn't care what he thought of it, she heard herself saying diffidently, 'I don't think I've got it quite right. I had terrible trouble with the bamboos in the foreground there.'

'It's — superb,' he said slowly. 'A wonderful present. Thank you.'

He was holding the picture away from him, to see it better, and she stared at it, seeing it really for the first time — the foreground of beach and trees, the blue shimmering hills beyond, and, in the centre, the tiny white doll's house that was Moon Creek. She felt a jarring shock as she realised just how much of herself had gone into it. Maybe not being a painter himself, though, he wouldn't realise this. She cleared her throat and forced a teasing smile to her lips.

'At least, if you've achieved nothing else while you've been here, you've made me go back to oils again.'

'Maggie, I — '

'I thought it would be a souvenir,' she

said brightly. 'Something for you to remember when you leave Moon Creek.'

'Oh, I shall never forget Moon Creek.' He too spoke lightly enough, but his eyes were sombre.

'Yes, well . . . ' She could *feel* him withdrawing from her. Even the painting had not bridged the gulf which had silently opened up between them. 'It isn't completely dry, so be careful with it for a few days.'

She yearned for him to take her in his arms, hold her all night to keep away the dark shadows that were circling round, just beyond the reach of the light, waiting for her. She gave him another brilliant smile. 'And now, if you don't mind, I'm very tired.'

He hesitated. Obviously, he felt some kind of responsibility for her, and she couldn't allow that. She walked across to the door and pulled it open.

'Goodnight, Steve.'

★ ★ ★

Maggie half opened her eyes then closed them again, wincing against the brilliant sunlight. She rolled over, then, catching sight of her silk dress lying on the chair where, hours before, she had thrown it, she buried her face in the pillow with a groan.

How *could* she have done it? After those encounters on the beach and in the attic, she'd sworn to keep away from him, not even to allow herself to think of him in that way. But then, born no doubt out of anger and misery, had come those other emotions which, if she allowed them, would sweep her away to destruction.

Her lips gave a bitter twist. At least, if it was any consolation, he was no doubt feeling exactly the same. What were they to do? The happy — or, at any rate, amicable — working atmosphere they'd managed to establish had been shattered once and for all under the frangipani trees, and there was no going back. But there was no going forward, either.

She lay, gnawing on her underlip, but

then, all at once, the solution plopped into her mind as neatly as a coin into a slot, and before she could change her mind she leapt up and went through to shower.

Fifteen minutes later, she was dressed and ready to go round to him. She'd already rehearsed what she would say. 'Look, Steve. There's no problem — we're both mature people — but we can't stay here together, not now. The way I'm working at the moment, I can paint anywhere, so I'll move out until you're ready to leave.' Pause for a few half-hearted protests. 'No, really, I don't mind. I might even go back to London for a while — I ought to see Marcus — and besides — well, we both know it's for the best, don't we?'

The glass door stood ajar, but when she went in he was not there; neither was he in the kitchen. She went upstairs, stood hesitantly outside his room and called, 'Steve?' But there was no answer and when, her heart beating nervously, she pushed the door open, the room was empty.

There was nothing of him there: nothing on the dressing-table, no clothes lying across a chair or — she opened it to check — inside the wardrobe, and the bathroom cabinet was empty. Only the faintest scent of his aftershave and the warm male smell that was him hung in the air — just for a few more hours. The bed hadn't been slept in — probably even before he'd left her he'd decided to go.

She went back downstairs, holding on to the banister very carefully. In the sitting-room there was nothing left of him, either — only a few crumpled pieces of discarded manuscript paper in the bin. She picked them out, smoothing the creases with great care, then, as she turned to go, she saw another crumpled piece on the top of the piano.

There was something heavy wrapped in it, and when she opened it the silver Gemini medallion and chain fell into her palm. Across the paper, in his bold, flowing hand, he had scribbled, 'Happy Birthday, Gemini'.

She stared down at it, seeing it dance and glitter through a sheen of tears. But she wouldn't cry — she'd vowed that she wouldn't. He'd known, like her, that they couldn't remain here together any longer, and he'd been very sensible, very considerate. Now there was no need for her to leave Moon Creek, and she hadn't really wanted to. So — it was for the best all round.

As she moved away from the piano, her hand brushed against some of the keys, and the soft sound fell into the room. It died away, and everything was still again.

It was strange, really, when you came to think about it. She'd cursed him often enough for being so big, so overpowering; he'd seemed to fill her part of Moon Creek as well as his own with his personality, his exuberance.

Now he was gone, and the silence was closing around her. She felt her face screw up, but then she walked out of the room, closing the door quietly behind her.

11

'Miss Maggie, do you want a drink? I've got you one.'

'Yes, please, Adela,' Maggie called and, laying down her brush, looked round to see the housekeeper come into the room, carrying a tray with a glass and a jug of iced lime juice.

Adela set it down on the table beside her then stood regarding her disapprovingly. 'Tch. You shutting yourself away in here too much, Miss Maggie. You getting so skinny — '

'Well, thank you,' Maggie put in ironically, but the housekeeper swept on.

'How you going to find a man to marry you if you go on like this? No husband, no babies.'

'Now, now, Adela.' She smiled teasingly at the older woman. 'There are other things in life besides husbands — and babies.'

'That's as maybe.' A loud sniff. 'But I hear you go to Hope's Mill yesterday, to see Miss Cathy that was.'

Maggie groaned inwardly. The island bush-telegraph at work again — reporting already on her visit to Cathy, her oldest friend, and her English husband and children on their latest trip back to the island. That magic circle of love which she'd felt and which had so disturbed her . . .

But how did Adela know? Of course, she was forgetting that she and Mattie, the housekeeper at Hope's Mill, were cousins, and that both of them, for nearly thirty years now, had been utterly devoted to the well-being of their respective charges.

'I hear you can hardly bear to put down Miss Cathy's new baby.'

'Oh, Adela!' Maggie gave a forced laugh. 'Sophie *is* my godchild, remember.'

Another loud sniff. 'I'm not forgetting, but godchild is not the same as — '

The telephone shrilled from the sitting-room.

'I'll take it, Miss Maggie.'

With a sigh of relief, she picked up her brush again, but within a few seconds Adela was back.

'It's for you — long distance.'

Maggie jumped to her feet. 'Who is it?'

'Didn't give his name — says he's from some art gallery.'

'Oh, it must be Marcus.'

But what on earth did he want? Not more flower studies, surely? She'd finally managed to complete the second assignment but, although he'd written to say he had been delighted with them, her heart hadn't been in the work and, if he wanted more, she knew she'd have to refuse.

'Hello — Marcus? Sorry to keep — '

'Miss Sanderson — Marguerite Sanderson?'

'Yes.' The voice was not Marcus', and the accent not his polished-over London cockney. Surely, it was — Her

248

fingers tensed on the receiver.

'You don't know me. My name's James Ellison — I run a gallery here in Boston.'

So she'd been right. A lighter timbre than Steve's, but — 'What can I do for you?' she asked guardedly.

A laugh. 'Well, it's more what we can do for each other, Miss Sanderson. One of your pictures came my way recently and I like it very much. I think there would be a market for your work up here.'

So Marcus hadn't liked those second studies, after all, and was disposing of them in single lots. She felt rather hurt, even though she'd known herself that they —

'I have some extremely wealthy clients, so I could promise you, I'm sure — '

Maggie roused herself. 'But I'm afraid I don't really work in water-colours any more. I'm awfully sorry if you — '

'Oh, this isn't water-colour. It's oils.'

249

But she hadn't sold any oil paintings — not to Marcus or anyone else. 'What is it of?' she asked slowly.

'It's a really fine painting in my opinion. You'll remember it, I'm sure. A landscape from your part of the world, I should think — beach, woods behind, and in the middle distance a small white house.'

Maggie's fingers clutched convulsively on the chair back she had been fidgeting with.

'I'm sorry, Miss Sanderson, I didn't catch that.'

'Oh — nothing,' she said quickly. So he hadn't even kept her picture. Oh, no doubt he'd hung on to it for a few weeks — after all, it had been a present, and one didn't give presents away lightly — but in the end he'd wanted to break even that last, tenuous link with her.

'Of course, I don't know how many others you have to hand — ' Maggie smiled grimly to herself, seeing in her mind's eye the endless stream of canvases she'd produced over the last three months, painting with a kind of feverish haste she'd never known before ' — but I was thinking along the lines of a small showing in the fall, and then a larger exhibition next spring or summer. I'm very tied up here at present, so I wondered if you'd care to come up for a few days — I'll be happy to meet your expenses, of course.'

'Oh — no. I couldn't possibly.' Go to *Boston*, of all the cities on the surface of the earth? 'No, I'm sorry,' she improvised desperately. They weren't at all Marcus' style, but — 'I already have links with a gallery in London, so I really think I should let them see my work first.'

'Well, I'm sorry.' He sounded genuinely regretful. 'Let me give you my phone number, at least. No, please — ' as she tried to protest ' — and I beg you to think it over. I truly believe that this could be a breakthrough for you.'

After she had put the phone down, Maggie sat for several minutes, her chin cupped on her hand, then got up and went back to the studio. She had left the tape recorder playing softly and she clicked the switch viciously, cutting off the guitar in mid-chord.

You fool, she thought savagely, you maudlin fool — you're still torturing yourself, still playing his music, when he can't even keep your painting. You've done it again, haven't you? Not content with letting one man give you a mauling, you've actually allowed another one to tear you apart. And this time you're not going to be able to put yourself together again, are you? But I must, she cried in silent anguish. I have to — I can't go on like this.

She banged the flat of her hand on the table. Oh, it was all utterly ridiculous. There'd been some excuse in David's case — after all, they'd been together six years — but to be like this for a man she scarcely knew, and disliked what she did know . . .

She'd reacted differently, of course; even when she'd found her chocolates hidden away in Steve's fridge, she'd felt no desire to gorge herself on them. So, how had she got over David? Work, in the end, had been her salvation. Well, she'd done plenty of that recently, but maybe she needed the ego boost of a market for her paintings — and she had to eat, after all, although she'd done precious little of that lately.

And now she'd turned down this golden chance. How many artists were lucky enough actually to have a dealer begging for their pictures? But she'd blown it, and just because the gallery was in Boston. It was a huge place, wasn't it? Quite big enough for her to lose herself in — and if she did see him, well, she could always run away. After all, he'd be doing exactly the same thing . . .

She reached for the scrap of paper on which she'd jotted down James Ellison's number.

*   *   *

'Do you know Boston at all?'

'No, I've never been here before. It looks really lovely.' Maggie turned to smile at the dark-haired man beside her in the front seat of the Buick.

'In that case, I hope you'll allow me to show you something of the city. A pity you can't be here for longer than just the one night — '

She murmured something about previous commitments.

'But at least you must let me buy you dinner, when we can continue discussing your work. By then, I'll have had a chance to look at these.' He gestured to the large, flat brown-paper package on the seat behind them. 'Then we could take in a movie, perhaps.'

'Oh, that would be nice, thank you.'

He'd assured her that her hotel was very pleasant, but even so, it would be a shame to spend her only night in Boston staring at the four walls of her room . . .

★ ★ ★

254

But when, a few hours later, he escorted her into the theatre, Maggie realised, with stunned disbelief, that it was no ordinary film that they were 'taking in'. When they finally broke through the jostling crowds, she glimpsed a poster proclaiming 'Charity Première', and she saw that the foyer was overflowing with beautiful, gorgeously dressed and bejewelled women, and their escorts in immaculate evening dress. Her eyes widened even more as, among the glamorous beauties and rugged profiles, she recognised faces familiar from television and the big screen, and from the gossip columns of glossy magazines.

She glanced sideways at Ellison, trying to suppress a faint twinge of annoyance. He was obviously trying to give her a treat, and the seats must have cost him a fortune, but even so she'd have felt considerably happier slipping into a slightly more down-market cinema rather than this exotic goldfish bowl. She was only grateful that, because they'd been going out to dinner first, she'd made an effort to dress up as well as she could.

Nervously, she looked down at her new dress and jacket in fine cream wool. At least, to go with the simple elegance of her outfit, she was wearing her hair in a more than usually sophisticated, upswept style. Even so, she picked at some imaginary fluff on her skirt before allowing herself to be guided through the scrum and into the huge auditorium.

As they took their seats, Ellison handed her an ornate souvenir programme, and she began flicking idly through it. Then all at once her fingers stilled, as she came face to face with a photograph of Steve.

He leaned against a piano, gazing back at her, dark eyes cool, that enigmatic half-smile quirking his mouth. Even in this black and white photograph she could detect that he had put up that façade of detachment which he was so good at. In the first few weeks after he'd left, she'd several times tried to paint a portrait from memory, but each time she'd given up in despair when she'd failed to capture anything of the real, elusive man.

What on earth — ? Feverishly now, she fumbled through the pages until she came to the list of credits, and read, with a sick plummet of the stomach, 'Score — Stefan Barshinsky'.

Panic flared in her. Did that mean that he was here? This, after all, was his home town and so surely he would —

'Look. Over there.' Maggie tensed as an excited whisper came from the row behind, then relaxed as the voice went on, 'Jude Renton — and surely that's Claudia Wexford.'

She allowed her eyes to swivel discreetly and, sure enough, there were the two stars of tonight's film making their way down through the auditorium, pausing at every other step to greet people they knew. How like their on-screen personae they looked . . . And then, a few yards behind them, ambling casually down the steps, in formal evening dress, his straw-coloured hair gleaming under the soft lights — Steve.

The spear thrust that ripped through her was so severe, so wholly unexpected, that she half closed her eyes, swaying slightly with the intensity of the pain. She sensed her companion's eyes on her and somehow managed a weakly reassuring smile in his direction, then stared straight ahead, her hands clenched in her lap until the nails dug into the flesh.

How could she have been such a blind fool? How could she, in all the previous weeks and months, not have recognised her feelings for what they were? Perhaps it was because she'd thought she'd loved David, and her feelings for Steve had been so overwhelmingly different that she'd been deceived by them. But now, as the blindfold tumbled from her eyes, she realised at last that she loved him, and that — way past all the quarrels and the fights — she had loved him ever since they'd first met.

The lights were going down, the hum of chatter died, and Maggie allowed herself to subside into the rescuing darkness. Afterwards, she couldn't have repeated a line of the screenplay, much less attempted even the baldest outline of the plot. Even the music, although she wanted desperately to hear it, still managed only to be a vague blur of sound somewhere beyond her consciousness. The only coherent thought was that, at all costs, she had to escape without his knowing that she was there.

As soon as the final credits rolled, almost before the lights started to come up, she turned to Ellison and under cover of the rapturous applause said, 'That was wonderful — ' she only remembered that bit just in time ' — but would you mind taking me back to my hotel now, please?'

'Sure. But wouldn't you like to stay on for a drink first?'

Stay on? Go through to the bar, where surely Steve and the others would be congregating to receive the congratulations and admiring plaudits?

'Oh, no, I'd really rather not. I — I have a bit of a headache.'

It wasn't a lie — a tight band was settling into place over her temples which would no doubt turn into a full-blown raging pain before very long.

'Of course.'

People were getting to their feet now, and so she allowed herself to be solicitously escorted out and through the brightly lit foyer.

'Oh, no, what a night,' Ellison exclaimed.

Earlier, it had been a fine early September evening; now, the rain was lashing the street, bouncing off the pavement. He turned to her.

'You wait here under cover, Maggie, and I'll get the car.'

She stood to one side as other people milled around her, spilling out through the doors, in their turn exclaiming over the weather and scrabbling in their bags for umbrellas. Every sense heightened, she seemed each moment to hear Steve's voice behind her, feel a detaining hand on her elbow, so that a rumble of thunder made her almost leap from her skin.

Where *was* James? So many people had hurried off into the night that she was beginning to feel dangerously exposed again. Ah, there was a car — a dark Buick — slowing over there. She heard a blast of the horn, saw a hand beckon. Yes, it was him. Thank heavens for that. She scurried across to the car, holding her programme over her head and, as the passenger door was pushed open, thankfully flung herself in.

The car moved off again and, laughing with sheer relief, she brushed the raindrops from her face. She turned to face the driver, then went very still.

'Hello, Maggie,' said Steve.

12

Steve did not look at Maggie; his eyes were on the moving stream of cars which he had notched into.

'How — ?'

But all her powers of speech had fled, swallowed up in the tidal wave of panic which had engulfed her, so that her only thought was that she had to escape. She caught hold of the door, but before she could throw it open he dragged her hand away.

'You little idiot. Don't try any damn-fool tricks like that.'

'Take me to my hotel.' Her voice was shaking, but at least she'd discovered how to use it again.

'And where might that be?' He still seemed to be giving most of his attention to the heavy after-première traffic.

'Don't give me that,' she snapped.

'You — you fixed all this, didn't you?'

'I might have.'

'In that case, you know very well that I'm staying at the Copley Plaza, and I insist that you take me there right now.'

'It seems to me you're in no position to insist on anything at the moment.'

Anger and frustration were taking over from her terror. 'I just hope your tame lap-dog is enjoying his walk home in the rain.'

Steve laughed. 'Jim, you mean? Well, this *is* my car he's been using all day — and I think he can just about afford the price of a cab.'

'But — but why have you done it?' She was bewildered. 'Why go through all this stupid charade?'

'Charade? What charade?'

'Getting your — friend to pretend that he's interested in my work.' On top of everything else, her realisation of this cruel deception was adding to her sense of desolation.

'Oh, that.' He shrugged carelessly. 'Well, I had to find some way of getting you up here. I knew if I called you you'd hang up on me, and a letter would go straight in the trash can.'

'Too right it would,' she said through her teeth.

'But I want to talk to you.'

Talk to her? There was nothing for either of them to talk about, ever again — especially not now, not after that moment of stunning self-revelation back there in the theatre. She knew that she had to break free from him, now, before the wounds were reopened any further, or the anguish of another parting would utterly destroy her.

'Well, as you see, I'm here,' she said bitterly. 'So, what do you want to say to me?'

'I've been thinking maybe it's time I had my portrait done for all my fans, and as you're the only painter I know — '

'I don't believe this. You've got me all the way up here, just to satisfy your inflated ego.'

Struggling to subdue the angry pain

at his casual cruelty, she stared out of the side window, then caught sight of a building she recognised. 'That's my hotel.'

'Really?'

She turned to him, but when she saw his implacable profile the pleading words died in her throat; she folded her arms tightly across her chest as though to hug herself into some kind of reassurance, and looked straight ahead, past the swishing windscreen-wipers, at the road, the traffic, the street lights — anywhere but at him.

The car turned into a wide, tree-lined boulevard and pulled up at the kerb. He got out, locked his door then came round and opened hers. 'Out.'

'Suppose I don't?'

'Maybe you'd like me to help you.'

To the group of passers-by, hurrying through the cascading rain, he must have seemed all solicitude, but as he caught hold of her arm she got out hastily and allowed herself to be steered up the steps of an old red-brick terraced house. He opened the door, ushering her in just as though she were an ordinary guest.

In the square hall, he shrugged off his lightweight mac and hung it on a peg. His back was to her and, as she took in that thatch of hair, now darkened by the rain, she saw them both again beneath the frangipani trees, her fingers lacing in that sun-bleached hair as she cried out his name and tumbled helplessly into the void. She curled her hands in her jacket pockets and clenched her teeth against the sick misery.

Attack was her only defence. 'You've got me here, Steve, but we haven't anything to say to each other — you must know that.'

He turned, and she looked away quickly, terrified that her expression would betray the hollowness of her words. He advanced on her, his hand outstretched.

'Your jacket's soaked. Give it to me.'
Reluctantly she took it off and he

hung it up, then led the way into a spacious sitting-room. He switched on the wall lights and, going over to the wide hearth, took up a poker and prodded into life the log fire that was burning low.

He straightened up, unhooked his tie, tossed his jacket on to a chair and threw himself down on the long, low sofa. 'Are you going to stay there all night?' he demanded.

When she still hovered in the doorway he scowled at her. 'Come in, for heaven's sake.'

As she closed the door and advanced two paces, he favoured her with a slow scrutiny. 'You've lost weight. You're too thin.'

She didn't need him to tell her that. 'Well, it's better than being round,' she snapped.

But he just smiled. 'That's a matter of opinion.'

'This is your house, I take it?'

'Of course.'

'So you haven't appropriated it from

your obliging friend *Jim* for the evening.'

'Oh, no. It's all mine,' he said blandly.

She wanted to show no interest, to stand there defiantly until he gave in and took her back to her hotel, but she could not resist the need at last to see his home territory, and she gazed round her. The enormous, high-ceilinged room — so appropriate for such a large man — was furnished with beautiful modern pieces in teak and leather. In the shadows at the far end was an old Steinway grand, and on the wall above it —

'It suits the room, don't you agree?'

He hadn't got rid of it, after all! She barely heard him for the utterly ridiculous somersaults of joy her heart was performing under her ribs.

'But — but,' she swung round to him, still half-accusing, 'James told me that he had it.'

Steve gave her a cat-like grin. 'Not exactly. I admit that Jim might have been a little — economical with the truth on that score, but everything else is genuine enough. He *does* own that Gallery in Newbury Street, and he never stops ogling that painting of yours. He's tried hard enough to wheedle it out of me, so I promised him that if he — uh — assisted me, I'd guarantee him a steady stream of Sanderson originals.'

'Oh.' Much of her outrage and indignation had been cut away from under her, but even so, 'You were very sure of me, weren't you?'

He met her gaze. 'Sure of you? Oh, no, Maggie — never.'

She looked across at him uncertainly. There seemed to be an utter seriousness in his words, but it was he, she reminded herself fiercely, who'd walked out on her — with not the slightest sign of concern for her, even though he'd known how bruised she already had been after David.

He leaned his head back and patted the cream leather. 'Come and sit by me.'

How tired he looked, and, all at once, so strained. Against all her reason, every fibre in her body ached to run to him and hold him in her arms, but instead she walked across and sat stiffly at the very end of the sofa, leaving two clear cushion-widths between them.

'Why *did* you get me up here, Steve?'

He paused fractionally. 'I was worried about you.'

'Worried?' She turned sharply to look at him. Whatever she'd expected, it wasn't this.

'Yes. At first — when I left,' he was looking not at her, but at his own slender fingers which were playing a tattoo on the leather, 'I was so engrossed in my own work that I managed — well, almost,' he gave her a wry smile, 'managed to shut you out. But then — I got worried.'

She set her head proudly. 'You needn't have done. I'm fine. After all, we — we neither of us wanted any commitment, did we?'

'No, you don't get my meaning,' he

said quietly. 'I thought, as we didn't take precautions that night — at least, I didn't, and I don't imagine you did — that you might be pregnant.'

So he'd fetched her all the way up here just to give himself the final reassurance that he had no moral obligation to her.

'Please don't worry any longer.' In spite of her rigid control, her voice quivered slightly. 'I can put your mind at rest right now. I'm not.'

'Ah.'

He nodded in acceptance of her words but his expression did not change. No doubt, though, he was breathing a sigh of relief. He wouldn't have wanted the complications of maintenance arrangements, stretching to infinity.

'Did you enjoy the movie this evening?'

'Oh, yes, it was wonderful' she said guiltily. 'Er — Jude Renton was marvellous, of course.'

'Of course,' he agreed gravely. 'And the music?'

'That was very good, too,' she said carefully.

'So glad you liked it.' She stirred uneasily under his sardonic gaze. 'Not too much — jingle-jangle for you?'

'Oh, no — not at all,' she stammered, her face colouring at the memory of her words that first evening on the veranda.

'Well, in that case, maybe you'd care to hear this other piece I've been working on.'

No, she wouldn't. All she wanted was to get away, but already, without waiting for her response, he was moving across to the Steinway. He adjusted the sheets of music that stood ready on the piano and began to play.

As the first silver notes filled the room, Maggie sank back into the sofa, captivated in spite of herself. The music was warm and joyous, and as she closed her eyes under its spell she felt herself being carried back to Moon Creek, so that she could almost feel the burning sun on her face, hear the waves sweeping in to a tropical shore.

Woven through it was a lyrical theme, which appeared and reappeared, alternately rapturous and throbbing, and then so tender that it brought an aching sadness to her heart, until at last it erupted into a storm of passionate urgency which finally died away.

Steve, his hands still resting on the keys, sat for a few moments with his back to her, but then he slowly swivelled round. 'Well, what do you think?'

He was watching her intently, and she struggled to free herself from the spell which the music had woven around her. She blinked back the tears and said huskily, 'It was wonderful.'

'Hmm.' Behind the non-committal grunt, though, she sensed a relief, a faint relaxing of tension. 'It'll sound better, of course, with a full orchestra, but perhaps you'd like to see the score.'

He went across to a side table, picked up a leather-bound volume and dropped it into her lap. Wonderingly, she opened it at the title page and read, 'A Summer

Rhapsody'; then, 'Stefan Barshinsky'; then, 'For M.S'.

'But why?' The letters shimmered through the haze of tears.

'It would never have been written if it weren't for you,' he said simply. 'I've been commissioned to produce an album from the film, and this is it! I was working on it that time I locked you up — remember?' He smiled wryly. 'And that other night — the night of my birthday.'

'Oh.'

Their glances met then skidded away.

'I guess I was trying to write out of me everything of you.' He reached out for her hand. 'That morning — I knew I had to get the hell out of Moon Creek. You — you'd taken me over, and I couldn't shake you off. I'd vowed, no commitment, but you were there in every part of my being, like a virus, so I tried to get rid of you by writing out all the feelings I had for you through the music.'

She heard again that soaring, lyrical

theme. 'F-feelings?' she whispered.

He was softly stroking his thumb across the back of her hand. 'Love.' Her whole body stiffened in shock. 'And anger — against you because of that love, which I'd tried so hard to reject.'

She could hardly trust herself to speak. 'So you wrote all those feelings out of you?'

'I actually thought I had. But then, out of the blue, it hit me that you might be pregnant. I was terrified that you were, and that if I asked you to marry me, you'd think, after all I'd said, that it was only out of some cold sense of duty.' He gave her a crooked little smile. 'At the same time, at the mere thought that you might be carrying my child I felt such aching tenderness for you that I knew I'd failed utterly. I hadn't cut you out of myself at all, and now I know I never will, while there's breath in my body.'

He put his hand under her chin, tilting her face to his. 'My darling Maggie, will you marry me?'

Dared she let this man into her life, permanently to cause chaos and havoc? She looked at him, seeing the lines of tension round his mouth, the intensity of his dark blue eyes, and she knew her answer.

'Yes, Steve, I will.'

'Oh, Maggie.'

He breathed out an enormous sigh of relief and enfolded her in his arms, holding her tight against his white shirt front. For long, timeless minutes she snuggled against him, feeling the waves of happiness wash through her, but then a tiny worry began to gnaw away at the back of her mind.

'Steve,' she murmured.

'Mmm?'

'Do you think — that is, won't we quarrel? We're both artistic, and — '

' — and Geminis, you mean?' He laughed softly into her hair and, reaching into the neck of her dress, drew out the silver medallion, letting it swing gently between his fingers.

'My darling, I'm quite sure we shall.

We'll yell at one another, throw things at one another, and sometimes even want to hurt one another. But it'll be all right, I promise you. Sometimes, though, I'll have to go away from you, to work,' he held her from him, his expression only half-teasing, 'because, when you're around I can only think about one thing — and it's not composition.'

'And what might that be? Do tell me.'

She gave him a provocative look from under her lashes, and he snatched her to him, his eyes darkening with desire, but then just as forcibly pushed her away.

'No.' He stood up and, putting out his hand, pulled her up beside him. As she pouted, he went on urgently, 'Don't look like that, Maggie. You know I can hardly keep my hands off you, and this time I'm determined to, at least — '

'At least?' she prompted.

' — until we're married. That's why I'm taking you back to your hotel now, and why I want you to move in tomorrow with my parents.'

'Your *parents*?'

'Yes. They live just three blocks away. Oh, don't look so alarmed, honey.' He stroked her hair tenderly.

'But — do you think they'll like me?'

He gave her a wry smile. 'I should think it more than likely. Only this morning, my mother yelled at me, 'Stefan, for heaven's sake, get that girl to marry you, and come back to the human race!' Oh, Maggie.'

He held out his arms to her and, as the love and longing welled up in her, she went into them.

13

'Oh, do stop here, please, Steve.'

Obediently he braked, and for several minutes they sat gazing down at the white house, shimmering in the hazy distance. He slid his arm round Maggie's shoulder.

'Happy?'

'Mmm. Of course.' She laid her head on his arm.

'And glad to be alone — at last.'

'Yes, but we couldn't disappoint them all — your family and mine.'

'No,' he agreed drily. 'Especially when they were all so determined to make it the Boston wedding of the year. It was great to meet your folks, though, even if your gran had to beat it to the airport even quicker than we did.'

Maggie smiled. 'Well, she did have that flight to catch.'

'Yes, of course. I'd hate for her to

have missed out on her camel safari across the Sahara.'

'Oh, don't be an idiot.' She laughed. 'You know it's nothing like that — they're going in perfectly good Land Rovers.'

'But I didn't have a real chance to thank her.'

'For giving us Moon Creek as a wedding present, you mean?'

'Well — that, and,' he put his thumb under her chin, gently pulling her face up to his, and at the expression in his eyes her insides melted in pure joy, 'for being the grandmother of such an enchanting, adorable young woman.'

His arms tightened around her, then he gently kissed her nose. 'We'd better get on down there.'

He slipped in the clutch and they rolled slowly on down the hill, to where Adela and the others were waiting.

Later, they ate dinner out on the veranda.

'Do you remember,' Maggie was pouring coffee, 'that first morning, when I came round to beg for a drink, you were out here, exactly in this spot?' She grinned impishly at him, her grey eyes glinting in the candlelight. 'I hope you're not wearing those highly patriotic boxer shorts.'

'No, I don't think so — but yes, I remember.' Steve, reaching for his cup, pulled a rueful face. 'That was the moment, if I needed any telling by then, when I realised that the pint-sized tornado with hair like golden flames, who'd pushed her way into my life a mile up over the Caribbean, spelled danger. But it was already too late. I think that was why I got so mad when your friend Reid couldn't come up with any alternatives. I knew inside me that if I didn't get away, and soon, I was doomed.' He drained his cup, stood and held out his hand. 'It's a wonderful evening — let's go for a walk.'

The soft tropical darkness closed around them as they followed the river down to the creek, gleaming pale silver in the moonlight, then round to the beach. They stood, side by side, watching the little waves shushing on to the sand, until at last they made their way back to the waiting house.

Maggie looked up at the first-floor windows. 'I hope you're not going to lock me up again, and not let me out till I've painted another picture.'

He laughed softly. 'No, I don't think so — not tonight, anyway. Tonight, I have other plans for you.'

At the unspoken meaning in his eyes, she felt the rose-pink rise in her cheeks and the pulse at her throat quicken, but still she managed to say casually, 'Hmm, well, that room with the bars — it does seem a waste to use it as a prison when it would make such a perfect nursery.'

He turned to her, and, raising her hand to his lips, gently kissed it, then, arms entwined, they went up the wide staircase.

Adela had prepared the big master bedroom at the front of the house. She had lit more candles, and draped across the bed was one of Maggie's trousseau nighties, a slip of lace-edged coffee silk, while on the pillow —

She went very still. What did it mean? Fertility, and happiness in bed, wasn't it?

Beside her, Steve said softly, 'Whose idea was that, do you think?'

'Joseph's, I imagine.' Her voice was husky. 'He's from one of the villages in the hills, where they keep up all the old traditions.'

'In that case, we mustn't disappoint him.'

He turned her to him and very carefully, with hands that ever so slightly trembled, unbuttoned her turquoise linen dress and dropped it at her feet. She heard his breath catch softly in his throat as he looked down at her, then he unclipped her bra to release the rosy fullness of her breasts, his fingers moving delicately across their yearning centres, and finally slid her panties from her.

'Oh, Maggie — you're so lovely,' he

said shakily, and gathered her to him.

As they stood there, wrapped in each other's arms, she felt the overpowering love and happiness rise in her. Gradually, though, the little flames of desire began to flicker through them both and she felt his body tense into life. He released her and, reaching for the frangipani garland, moved her hair aside and placed it round her neck. Then he lifted her into his arms again, laid her on the bed, and came down beside her.

Outside, the night was silent and still. In their charmed circle of candlelight, though, as their bodies twined, they sighed and whispered endearments, until the scented flowerlets fell from the wreath and gently drifted to the floor.

THE END

We do hope that you have enjoyed reading this large print book.

Did you know that all of our titles are available for purchase?

We publish a wide range of high quality large print books including:
Romances, Mysteries, Classics
General Fiction
Non Fiction and Westerns

Special interest titles available in large print are:
The Little Oxford Dictionary
Music Book, Song Book
Hymn Book, Service Book

Also available from us courtesy of Oxford University Press:
Young Readers' Dictionary
(large print edition)
Young Readers' Thesaurus
(large print edition)

For further information or a free brochure, please contact us at:
Ulverscroft Large Print Books Ltd.,
The Green, Bradgate Road, Anstey,
Leicester, LE7 7FU, England.
Tel: (00 44) **0116 236 4325**
Fax: (00 44) **0116 234 0205**

Other titles in the
Linford Romance Library:

DANGER COMES CALLING

Karen Abbott

Elaine Driscoe and her sister Kate expect their walking holiday along Offa's Dyke Path to be a peaceful pursuit — until a chance encounter with a mysterious stranger casts a shadow of fear over everything. Their steps are constantly crossed by three men — Niall, Steve and Phil. But which of them can they trust? And what is the ultimate danger that awaits them in Prestatyn?

NO SUBSTITUTE FOR LOVE

Dina McCall

Although recently made redundant, nurse Holly Fraser decides to spend some of her savings on a Christmas coach tour in Scotland. When the tour reaches the Callender Hotel, several people mistake Holly for a Mrs MacEwan. Furthermore, Ian MacEwan arrives to take her to the Hall, convinced that she is his wife, Carol! Although Ian despises Carol for having deserted him and their two small children, two-year-old Lucy needs her mother. Holly stays to help the child, but finds herself in an impossible situation.

LOVE'S SWEET SECRETS

Bridget Thorn

When her parents die, Melanie comes home to run their guest house and to try to win the Jubilee Prize for her father's garden. But her sister, Angela, wants her to sell the property, and her boyfriend, Michael, wants a partnership and marriage. Just before the Spring opening, Paul Hunt arrives and helps Melanie when the garden is attacked by vandals. After the news is splashed over the national papers, guests cancel. Then real danger threatens. But who is the enemy?